CW00923520

ONE-TIMER

TEAGAN HUNTER

Copyright © 2022 by Teagan Hunter

All rights reserved. For your personal enjoyment only. This book may not be re-sold or given away to other people. If you did not purchase this book, or it was not purchased for your use only, please return it and purchase your own copy. Thank you for not pirating and respecting the countless hours the author has put into this book.

This book is a work of fiction. Names, characters, businesses, places, events, and incidents are either the products of the author's imagination or used in a fictitious manner. Any resemblance to actual persons, living or dead, or actual events is purely coincidental.

No part of this book may be reproduced in any form or by any electronic or mechanical means, including information storage and retrieval systems, without written permission from the author, except for the use of brief quotations in a book review. To obtain permission to excerpt portions of the text, please contact the author at teagan@ teaganhunterwrites.com.

Editing by Editing by C. Marie

Proofreading by Judy's Proofreading & Julia Griffis

Cover Design: Emily Wittig Designs

To Tash Drake.
You'll be missed so much.

.

CHAPTER 1

HOLLIS

Weddings are supposed to be happy days. They are supposed to be filled with smiles and love and tears of joy.

Weddings are not supposed to be filled with infinite sadness and enough tears to fill a damn decorative mason jar.

But here I am, sitting in my car, crying my eyes out because my little sister is marrying the love of her life this weekend and I just signed my divorce papers earlier this week.

I can't force myself to get out and face it all.

Don't get me wrong, I am beyond thrilled for my little sister. Harper has always been a cynic when it comes to love, so the fact that she's about to walk down the aisle and exchange vows is monumental. It's an even bigger deal because she's marrying NHL superstar Collin Wright, but that's a whole different conversation.

Watching her get a perfect life she never really wanted when I was the little girl who planned her wedding at five years old and thought I had found my happily ever after? Yeah, it stings.

Not nearly as much as finding out your husband had a mistress and they'd been sleeping together *before* you got married, but it still stings.

I swipe at the tears running down my cheeks, frustrated by them—my tears and my ex-husband and his mistress. As embarrassing as it was when Harper came home to tell my mother and me she was engaged, I cried then too. In front of her. Like straight up just burst into tears like an awful big sister.

After that whole mess, there is no way I can walk inside looking like this.

Another tear slips down my cheek, and I swipe at it. I am *not* about to ruin my sister's big weekend with my silly tears.

An old beat-up truck blasting music so loudly it's rattling my windows comes careening into the parking lot, whipping into the space next to mine as if it belongs here. I know for a fact it does not.

My brows slam together in frustration because the jerk doesn't even bother turning the music down. Doesn't he know two people who are madly in love are inside about to rehearse a ceremony so tomorrow they can start a new life together?

Ugh.

A set of fresh tears streaks down my cheeks at the thought. I squeeze my eyes shut, trying to push away the thoughts of what I've lost, then wipe at my face again, which I'm sure is a mess. I pull down the sun visor to check the tiny mirror inside and—yep, I'm a mess. Streaks of black run down my cheeks and a mess of makeup sits under each eye. All because my favorite mascara wasn't available in waterproof because *of course* it wasn't.

It's not a big surprise though. Nothing has gone right since I was blindsided by my cheating ex-husband.

My car was backed into, and the driver took off...in a parking lot that had *no* cameras.

I was detained for shoplifting because the cashier didn't want to believe me that the candy bar wrapper in the cart wasn't mine and I was feeling petty enough to argue.

Oh, and that haircut I treated myself with? Butchered, leaving me with a short bob, which I did *not* want.

It's been a challenging couple of months, to say the least.

The only positive is that this divorce hasn't been dragged out any longer than necessary. Thad granted me the divorce when he realized I had copies of his text messages. You'd think, being a lawyer, he would have done a better job of covering his tracks, but nope. He left everything out, right there for me to see. A part of me wonders if he did it on purpose. The way he acted in the months leading up to our wedding—like how he wasn't invested in the planning and was picking fights—should have been a red flag, but I was too caught up in the years

I'd put into our relationship and what I wanted for my future to see it for what it was.

Lies.

All big lies.

I should have listened to my best friend, Emilia, when she said Thad was a douchebag who wasn't to be trusted. Sure, she said it when she was drunk, but there's truth to our intoxicated ramblings, right?

"His name is Thad, Hollis. That should tell you everything you need to know about the douchebag."

In hindsight, she was right.

I wish she were here now. She always makes me laugh. But I have to suffer through tonight alone.

Tomorrow, though…tomorrow we drink. And then drink some more. I already know I'm going to need it.

With a sigh, I reach across my BMW—a hush gift from Thad since he didn't want his transgressions getting back to his buddies at the firm—to pop open the glove box.

And…nothing.

Not a damn thing.

"The one time I don't have ten billion Starbucks napkins shoved in there…"

I slam it closed, then lean my head back against the seat, trying not to cry yet again. I don't need an even bigger mess to clean up.

"Ugh. Get ahold of yourself, Hollis. You're acting ridiculous. It's just a napkin. That's it. It's a napkin."

Tears sting my eyes again because it's not *just a napkin*

—it's a wedding too, a wedding I am certainly going to bawl my way through, and not exactly for all the right reasons.

I squeeze my eyes shut to block out all the negative thoughts that are hurtling their way through my mind and take a deep breath.

Then another.

And one—

"OH MY GOD!"

I glare over at the old truck next to me, that damn music *still* rattling my windows. With the dents and scratches and the bumper hanging on by what looks to be a thread of duct tape, I don't understand how the truck itself hasn't rattled apart with how loud the music is.

The windows are tinted, but not so dark that I can't see inside. The driver is leaned back in the seat without a care in the world, a pair of dark sunglasses covering his eyes, looking like he's not moving anytime soon.

Is this asshole serious?

It's annoying. *He's* annoying.

I bet Harper and Collin must be inside right now wondering what the hell that loud, obnoxious noise is. I'll be damned if this asshole is going to ruin my little sister's rehearsal.

I shove my car door open, march to the driver's side of the asshole's truck, and smack my palm against the window.

He doesn't move.

What the…

I smack the window again.

No reaction. Not even a flinch.

Is this idiot sleeping?

I smack the window a third time and…nothing.

I huff, rolling my eyes skyward. Then, because I am off my rocker completely, I knock one last time—only there is no window, and I connect with the stranger's face, knocking his sunglasses askew.

I…I just hit a person!

"Oh shit!" I squeak out, retracting my hand and slapping it over my mouth.

I just got a divorce, my life is in shambles, I just hit a person, and now I'm probably going to jail for assault. Can my life get any worse right now?

The guy—who looks vaguely familiar, but I can't quite place him—works his jaw back and forth from the unexpected hit. He brings his large hand up, his long fingers caressing the spot where my palm connected with his face. His chest rises and then falls with a heavy sigh.

I hold my breath as he slowly—like at a glacial-pace slow—pulls his aviator sunglasses down and pierces me with the most dazzling green eyes I have ever seen. They're so unique and beautiful that I audibly gasp.

Luckily, preventing even further embarrassment, my hand is still firmly over my mouth, so I doubt he hears it.

His gorgeous eyes that are the color of pine narrow, and even that's not enough to get me to stop staring into them. They are so different than anything I've ever seen before. It's not the color that makes them so unique. It's the pain and secrets that are hiding within the swirls that make them stand out. This guy has been through things that have hardened him.

A sympathetic frown pulls at my lips because I can understand. I've been through things that have hardened me too.

"Are you fucking serious?"

And just like that, my sympathy is gone.

His tone is sharp and dark. And yeah, okay, he might have a reason to be pissed since I did just technically hit him, but still—he's the asshole who came barreling into the parking lot when there's a damn wedding rehearsal inside. Rude on its own, but especially rude since he doesn't even belong here.

"I'm dead serious. Your shitty taste in music is loud and disruptive and you have no business being here."

It's not shitty taste in music. I love the song. Everyone loves the song that's playing. It's a crime to not love Queen, but I'm not about to admit that to the jerk.

He lifts a dark brow. "That so?"

"That's so. This is a private event."

"Private event, huh?"

"Yes, and—"

He scoffs…then hits the button to roll his window back up, effectively cutting me off.

My jaw slackens as I stare at the truck, watching him disappear again.

Who the hell does this guy think he is?

I'm about to bang on the damn thing again, but I

don't have the chance. The loud rumble of his vehicle abruptly dies, and he pushes the door open. I jump back so I don't get whacked with it, though I guess it would be fair if I did get hit.

He slides out of the truck and towers over me. He's so tall I literally have to tip my head back to look up at him. He reaches up and turns the baseball cap on his head backward, and I'm annoyed with myself for finding the action even remotely attractive, especially since this guy is a total tool.

Even though he's wearing those damn aviator sunglasses again, I can *feel* his heated stare. I glare right back, crossing my arms over my chest, refusing to back down. I try not to think about how ridiculous I likely look right about now. I stand at least six inches shorter than him even though I'm wearing heels and am all dolled up in a tea-length dress for the rehearsal.

"This is a *private* event. What part of *private* are you not comprehending?"

I point back at the sign that clearly says the parking lot is closed, but he doesn't seem to care.

No.

His lips twitch.

He's amused, and that pisses me off even more.

He leans back against his dirty old truck and crosses his arms over his chest like he's settling in and not planning to leave when he's clearly not supposed to be here. "I guess all of it. Can you explain what the word private means?"

I scoff. "It means you're not invited. You don't belong here."

He nods. "And how exactly do you know I don't belong here? For all *I* know, it's *you* who doesn't belong here."

I wave a hand down my outfit. "My attire says otherwise."

"I see, and why is your attire so important?"

"Ha!" I point a finger at him. "If you belonged here, that wouldn't even be a question. You'd know exactly why I'm dressed like—"

"Like you have a stick up your ass?"

For the second time since I met this man, I audibly gasp at his words.

A stick up my ass?

Thad used to get upset whenever I wore something too low-cut to one of the many client dinners we had to attend. I learned fast that I didn't want to rock that boat and should cover up.

I never thought my wardrobe screamed *stick up my ass* though.

I narrow my eyes at him, choosing to ignore his jab. "You need to leave before I call security."

I have no clue if this place has security, but he doesn't know I don't know.

He laughs, and it's a low, deep sound. "Go ahead. Call them."

I don't like the confidence in his words. He sounds way too sure that there is nobody I can call.

"I will."

"Good. I'll wait."

He sinks back against the truck even more, watching me.

Waiting.

And waiting.

"Well?" he asks, arching a brow. "Are you going to call?"

"I don't have my phone."

"That's okay. You can use mine."

He reaches into his back pocket and produces the latest iPhone, holds it my way. I stare down at it with surprise, the device the sheer opposite of what he's driving. He doesn't look like he should have the latest anything, not when his truck is literally being held together with—holy crap, are those zip ties around the mirror?

"Go ahead. Call." He shakes his phone at me. When I don't reach for the device, a slow grin pulls at his lips. "Oh, I see. You were never going to call. You were just trying to scare me off, huh?"

"No. I'll call."

He wiggles the phone again, and I don't take it.

He lets out another low laugh, then slips the phone into his back pocket. His arms go back over his chest, and his stupid lips are pulled into a stupid grin. "Listen, darlin', I—"

"I am *not* your *darlin'*. I'm not your anything." I stalk toward him, lips curled at the unwanted nickname, and I don't stop until I'm just a few feet away, my finger pointed firmly at him. He doesn't look the least bit scared. In fact, he looks amused that he's riled me up, and it pisses me off even more. "You're trespassing at a private event, and I'm—"

He holds a hand up, stopping me. "Let me get this straight. You hit me, and *you're* mad at *me*?"

"I didn't hit you on purpose! And the only reason I hit you at all is that I was trying to get you to turn down your damn music because this is a private event and you're—"

"Let me guess...I'm trespassing?" He shakes his head, then pushes off the truck, leaning down until we're eye level. Our noses are nearly touching at this point, and I should be totally freaked out because this guy is a stranger. But I'm not. I'm too angry to be freaked out.

I also shouldn't be noticing that his bottom lip is bigger than his top or how soft his lips look.

But I do.

Just for a second.

Then, he opens those lips, and all thoughts of anything other than anger fly out the window.

"Well, I have news for you, *darlin'*: I'm not trespassing. I—"

The doors of the venue swing open, pulling our attention.

"Oh my gosh! You're here!" My little sister claps her hands, bouncing on her heels excitedly, the biggest smile on her face. I can't help but grin back at her. Collin stands just behind her, hands in his pockets, watching her with a smile on his face as she zips down the stairs toward me.

Harper pulls me into a hug, and I squeeze her back, melting into her warmth. For a moment, I almost forget about everything that's just happened and the jerk standing a few feet away from me.

She pulls back, looking me over. "You look…"

"Like a mess? I know." I wipe at the mascara that's pooled under my eyes. "Sorry. It's kind of been an emotional morning."

A sympathetic smile pulls at her lips, and I hate it. I don't want her sympathy.

Especially not this weekend.

I wave a hand. "Enough about that. I'm so happy for you, Harper."

Her sad smile turns radiant just like that.

"Thank you. I'm so happy for me too. And I'm so happy you two have already met," she says, nodding toward the guy standing behind us.

"Glad you found it," Collin says, clapping him on the shoulder and bringing me back to reality.

"Almost didn't." The guy smirks when he says it, and it's like they're in on some secret the rest of us don't know.

"Why is it good we've met?" I ask, looking around at the three of them, not understanding how they all know one another.

"This is Collin's teammate who you'll be walking

down the aisle with, duh. Now come on," she says, looping her arm in mine and dragging me toward the building. "You guys are late and we have some practicing to do."

This is my partner for the weekend?

This guy? The one I just punched in the face?

He's a pro-hockey player?

I glance back at him, watching as he slowly ambles up the stairs behind us, that smug grin he can't seem to wipe off firmly in place.

Fuck my life.

CHAPTER 2

Collin is lucky he's like a brother to me because otherwise, there is no way in hell I would ever put up with this shit.

First I have to spend the entire weekend with my teammates in the off-season. Don't get me wrong, I love these guys, but I also love my me time. And now he's telling me I have to spend the weekend with the girl who punched me in the face just minutes ago.

Sure, I was in the wrong for pulling into the parking lot with my music blaring like a maniac, but I don't think that warranted being hit in the face by a stranger.

Especially not in the parking lot of my own business.

I glance over at my attacker. She has her head thrown back laughing at something Emilia, the team's social media manager, is saying.

Looking at her now without all the mascara running down her face and the crazed look in her eyes, it's clear I should have picked up on the fact that this is Harper's sister. It's obvious they're related. Their faces are the same shape, and they have the same full lips, the same pert nose. Hell, even their hair color is the same shade of brown. They look like they could be twins instead of having the two-year age gap I know is between them.

And how do I know all this information? Collin. The dude never shuts up about his wife-to-be. But I suppose that's to be expected when you find your person.

I thought I had found my person once upon a time. Oh, how wrong I was. So very, very, embarrassingly wrong.

Hollis must feel my gaze because she glances over at me, and that smile she was wearing is replaced by a deep frown in a matter of milliseconds. The change is so drastic it makes me laugh. Which of course pisses her off even more. It's like she's annoyed by my mere existence.

She glares at me, and my smile pulls even wider. I chuckle when she turns her back to me completely.

We did several run-throughs for the wedding tomorrow, and each time I had to link arms with Hollis, she grew stiffer and stood farther away from me. It didn't take long for Harper to pick up on it, and she pulled Hollis aside. I have no idea what they talked about, but when we ran through it for the fourth time, it was much smoother.

Now that we're done practicing, Hollis is back to being ice cold. Funny, because I should be the one who is upset given the circumstances of our introduction.

"Having fun yet?"

My teammate Rhodes slides up next to me. He takes

a sip from his champagne glass, then lets out a long sigh like he's as exhausted by all of this as I am. Which is even funnier knowing that out of all of us, he's the one who has been married the most times.

I glance at the scar on his face, and I momentarily feel bad because even after all this time of knowing him, it's still the first thing my eyes drift to. I guess when you have a scar from right under your eye down your cheek and slicing through your lips *and* it's as marred and jagged as his, it's kind of expected.

If he notices, he doesn't say anything. Instead, he takes another drink, looking out at the small crowd in front of us. There aren't many people, only around twenty-five, but it feels like a hundred with how badly I don't want to be here right now.

I grunt in response to his question.

He laughs. "You look like you're having about as much fun as I do in crowds."

One of our best defensemen on the Carolina Comets, Adrian Rhodes isn't exactly known for being social. He's as notorious for skipping out on interviews as he is for his stats on the ice. He doesn't do press, and he certainly doesn't do crowds.

Hell, before his wife, Ryan, came along, we had to fight tooth and nail to get the dude to go have a beer with us—his own teammates—after a game. While we do still have to coax him into coming out more often than not, there have been many times in the last year that he's said yes without us prodding too hard.

But still, the dude hates crowds. For me, it's not so much the crowds; it's just the event.

"I'm just glad Ryan didn't make me wear a tie. I get enough of that during the season."

Fuck, he's telling me. If I could burn my suit and tie, I would. I know some guys love dressing up for games, but I am not one of them. Which is exactly why I wore a pair of dark jeans and a button-up shirt. I already have to dress up for this event tomorrow. I'm not doing it today too.

"Man, I'm glad we never had to go through all this formal shit for our wedding."

"I mean, to be fair, you did get married in Vegas…twice."

He grins like he's thinking back on it. "And I'd do it again in a heartbeat."

"Even the first time?"

"*Especially* the first time. It led me to Ryan."

I grimace at the lovey-doveyness of it all.

Rhodes takes notice and chuckles at my discomfort. "You know, it's kind of funny that as a guy who hates relationships so much, you co-own one of the hottest wedding venues with your sister."

"Trust me, I see the irony in it as well."

Not too long ago, my younger sister, Stacie, came to me with the idea of opening a wedding venue next to the brewery we own together in my hometown, which just happens to be about two hours from the arena I play at.

I'll admit, it took some convincing for me to be on

board with the wedding venue idea. We're a brewery—why did we need to host weddings? But when it became clear to me that it was something she was passionate about, I thought it was fair that I support her. After all, she gave up a lot of her childhood for my dreams and aspirations of playing professional hockey.

So, we tossed up a new building and connected the two with a huge outdoor seating area that's easily transformed into the perfect outdoor reception setting.

I never thought I'd be hosting my teammate's wedding here, but Harper fell in love with the place not even knowing it was my business since it's not really something I advertise. I'm more of a silent co-owner, especially during the hockey season. She was more than thrilled when I gave them the friends and family discount—meaning I didn't charge them a dime—on the venue. So, for them to be torturing me with all this other bullshit is really unfair.

It's nothing against Collin and Harper. I'm happy for them. What they have seems to be one of the rare occurrences—something real. Just like what Ryan and Rhodes have.

No, my problem has to do with my disdain of relationships in general.

Love and me? We don't get along too well.

My sister thinks I'm being stubborn and that I need to just move on. That's easy for her to say. She wasn't the one who was tricked into believing she got a woman pregnant, proposed, announced to the world he proposed, then found out it was all fake and nothing but a trap to get his pro-hockey money.

A trap I fell right fucking into too.

The worst part? I actually thought I was in love with her…and I know I was in love with the baby that never existed. I didn't just mourn the loss of my relationship; I mourned the loss of a future that was never really mine, and I am not about to hurl myself into another relationship. Getting burned like that once was enough for me, thanks.

So I keep it light and casual in that department. The one-timer isn't just good for the ice. It's pretty much how I get by.

"Okay, serious question, did anyone else notice the lack of babes at this thing?"

We both turn toward Miller, who is scanning the crowd with a frown.

"First"—Rhodes smacks him across the back of his head—"no. Stop trying to pick up women. Second, don't say *babes*. It's weird."

"First, *ow*. You ass." Miller rubs at the spot. "Second, I'm not trying to pick up women right now. I'm just scouting."

"Scouting?"

"For tomorrow," he elaborates.

I roll my eyes. "You're exhausting."

"And horny. So very horny. Lonely too."

"Yeah, but I'm sure your right palm isn't," Rhodes

comments, not even bothering to hide his smirk behind his champagne flute.

"Exactly! That's my problem." He holds said hand up. "It's getting tired. I'm pretty sure it's calloused —look!"

"I'd really rather not discuss your masturbation issues, Miller," I say to him.

"Would you rather talk about why you were late? Were *you* the one masturbating?"

I glare at him. "Hardly."

Not that I'd ever admit as much to the idiot, but I can sympathize with him. My dick has seen my palm more than it's seen a pussy in the last year or so.

But that's been by choice. After winning the Cup, I wanted to take another run at it, and I knew I couldn't get us far if I didn't focus. So that's what I did. I played hockey and took every other distraction off the table.

Clearly, it wasn't enough. We got knocked out of the playoffs in the second round.

But I don't want to dwell on that now.

"Why *were* you late though?" Rhodes asks. "Didn't want to come?" *Bingo.* "Even I beat you here, which never happens. You're always first."

He's right; it's not like me to flake on stuff. I'm usually the first on the ice in the morning and the last to leave every day and after every game.

"Got held up in the parking lot."

He cocks a questioning brow. "The parking lot? Here?"

"Yep. Don't you know I'm trespassing?"

I feel like I should be more upset about the whole encounter, but thinking back on how utterly insane Hollis looked standing outside my window with mascara streaks running down her cheeks, I can't help but laugh.

"On your own property?" Rhodes asks, looking just as confused as I was when I was accosted.

"Apparently so."

"That sounds…"

"Completely crazy? Yeah, I know. Tell that to the nut who assaulted me in the parking lot."

"Someone assaulted you in the parking lot?"

"Not just any someone. Harper's sister."

Miller—in his typical dramatic fashion—gasps. "No way."

"Yep. Clocked me right in the face."

"So, I know she's supposed to be your girl and all, so you get first dibs, but does this mean you don't have a chance with her? Is she available, then?" Rhodes and I both give him an incredulous look. "What? She's hot!"

"Hot or not, she's crazy."

He shrugs. "Crazy can be fun."

"What is wrong with you? I just told you she assaulted me."

"Oh my gosh! I did not *assault* you! It was an accident!"

I turn around to find Hollis standing there. She has one hand on her hip, her lips pressed tightly together as she stares down at me with eyes full of ire.

21

I lied earlier when I said she's dressed like she has a stick up her ass. Yeah, sure, her dress covers all of her assets and then some, but it definitely hugs her in all the right places too. It's sexy in an understated sort of way, especially now that she's washed her makeup off.

Frankly, she's beautiful, and it's distracting as hell.

And annoying, because I don't *want* to find her attractive. She's crazy.

Huh. Maybe Miller has a point about crazy after all…

"You really did hit him?" Miller holds his hand up to high-five her. "Nice! He probably deserved it."

She ignores his hand, keeping her eyes on me. "I obviously didn't know who you were."

"And you didn't bother trying to find out either. You just assumed I didn't belong. Why? Because of my vehicle?"

"That thing is a total piece of shit," Rhodes chimes in.

I'll admit it—my truck isn't in the best of shape. But it's the same damn truck I've had since the moment I turned sixteen, and I'm not ready to let her die yet. Even though I can afford a better vehicle—hell, I could afford multiple better ones—I can't give her up. She's been good to me, and I feel like I owe it to her to keep her going.

"I—I…" she sputters. "Well, I—"

"You what? Judged me? Jumped to conclusions?"

"No! Yes!"

"Well, which is it? No or yes?"

"Both."

"Tell me, do you assault everyone who you don't know based on the conclusions you've jumped to? You know, come to think of it, there was a lot of force behind that punch. Seemed kind of premeditated to me."

Her eyes narrow, her hand balling up at her side. "Oh, trust me, if I'd meant to hit you, you'd know it."

I don't know this woman at all, but something tells me she just might be telling the truth. She might appear to be a little buttoned up, but from that spitfire attitude she showed out in the parking lot, I'd say she's anything but.

"Somehow I doubt that, *darlin'*," I find myself saying just to taunt her.

The way her jaw works back and forth is a sign she doesn't like that one bit.

Now, normally, I have really good reflexes. You don't become an NHL player without them. I can usually read people really well. Again, pro-hockey player. It's just a skill set that comes with playing the game.

But nowhere, not once in all my years of training and playing a sport professionally, have I ever been prepared for this moment.

As if it's happening in slow motion and I'm in the audience watching it unfold on the big screen, Hollis lifts her champagne flute…and splashes the liquid directly in my face.

Miller and Rhodes jump back just in time, leaving me standing there soaked and pissed off.

Hollis takes a step toward me, her eyes cloudy and angrier than I've seen them yet—which is saying something. When she pushes up on her toes, our noses are nearly touching.

It's then that I notice one key difference between her and Harper—their eyes.

Pools of dark blue filled with rage stare back at me.

But it's not just any dark blue, and it's not just rage. There's a deep lonely sadness swimming in there too.

For a moment, a part of me forgets everything that happened in the parking lot and that I'm covered in champagne. For a moment, all I feel is complete empathy for her. I know what that deep sadness feels like, and I don't like that she's feeling it.

"I. Am not. Your. *Darlin'*."

Hollis spins on her heel and stomps away, the entire room bouncing their eyes between me and her retreating back, trying to figure out what the hell just happened.

"Dude," Rhodes hisses in my ear. "What the fuck did you do to her?"

I run my hand down my face to wipe it clean, shaking the excess champagne off my fingers. A few guests glare at me for getting droplets on them, but I don't really care. Apparently, I have a bigger problem.

"I think I just pissed off my date for the weekend."

"Yeah, I'd say." He lets out a humorless laugh. "Incoming."

He dips his head toward the other side of the room where Collin is charging my way as his soon-to-be wife beelines for the exit, running after her sister. He doesn't stop until he's directly in front of me, his nose flaring with anger. I've only seen him like this one other time, and that time, he landed himself in handcuffs.

I hold my hand up to stop him. "Save it. I'm not in the mood."

He steps toward me anyway, ignoring my hand. "I don't give two shits if you're in the mood or not. I also don't care what that was all about. All I care about is that you fucking fix it and you fucking fix it fast."

With a sigh, I give him one terse nod, then head in the same direction Harper and Hollis went, trying my best to ignore all the curious stares and murmurs from the other guests.

Part of me understands his frustration with me. If somebody came to my sister's wedding and screwed it up like I just did, I'd probably react the same way.

But none of this is actually my fault. *I'm* not the one who was acting like a crazy person. *I'm* not the one who was judging whether or not somebody belonged here. *I'm* not the one who was hitting. *I'm* not the one who threw champagne in somebody's face.

Okay, fine. I poked and prodded a bit, but still. Little dramatic, no?

I step into the hallway, and my eyes immediately go to two figures at the end of it. Hollis and Harper are huddled together, Harper with her arms around her big sister, consoling her. Hollis is crying, that much is obvious. Her shoulders are shaking with her sobs, and they aren't exactly quiet.

I'm starting to suspect I had very little to do with her outburst in both the parking lot and just now. It makes me feel bad because something else is clearly going on.

The strangest urge to walk down the hall and comfort her comes over me, and it stops me dead in my tracks.

My shoes squeak against the floor, and Harper's eyes meet mine at the sound. She narrows her eyes, shaking her head to stop me from coming any closer. She pulls away from Hollis, then mutters something to her that I can't quite make out from here. Whatever she says, it has Hollis nodding and wiping at her eyes.

Hollis gives her sister one last squeeze before rushing out the front door without so much as a backward glance. Harper watches her go for a moment before turning on me and stalking back down the hallway with the angriest look I've ever seen from her. She only stands at around five foot five, tiny compared to my six-foot-three stature, but fuck is she scary-looking right now.

I open my mouth to apologize to her, but when she holds her hand up, I snap it closed.

"Whatever apology or dispute you're about to send my way, save it for Hollis tomorrow. She's going through a lot right now and doesn't need any more drama tonight." She takes another step toward me. "But if I find out tomorrow that you did not apologize to my sister, there will be hell to pay, and I watch a lot of horror movies, so I know a lot of good places to hide a body where they won't find you for years."

I don't really doubt that she's telling the truth.

So, I nod. "Understood."

"Good. Now let's get back to the party. For, you know, my *wedding* tomorrow."

With one last glare, she brushes past me.

And I know this long weekend just got a whole lot longer.

CHAPTER 3

"Oh my gosh, you should have *seen* the way you two walked down the aisle. You were so stiff! I still can't believe you hit him."

"He deserved it! You could have warned me about him, you know," I gripe to Emilia as we slide up to one of the many bars this place has.

"Oh, come on. He's not that bad," she says. "In fact, he's actually really nice. Probably one of the nicer guys on the team if I'm being honest. He's always game for charity stuff, and he's *so* good with all the kids."

"You sound like you have a crush on him."

"Ha. Hardly. I mean is the man insanely hot? Yes. Obviously. Duh. But you don't want to mess around with hockey players." She says it like she's speaking from experience, and I have a feeling she is.

Emilia moved out here a couple of years ago after she discovered her boyfriend was living a double life with her and the neighbor next door. Much like me, she had to bail. Though I missed her, I couldn't blame her for doing it. Especially not when she was offered a social media manager position with a professional hockey team.

The very first weekend she lived here, she had a two-night stand with a mystery guy, and something in my gut tells me it was one of the players she works with, though she won't confirm it.

"Wait…it's not *him*, is it?"

"Uh…no." Though her cheeks flush a bright red. "Order me a wine, will you? I'm going to run to the bathroom really quick."

I plop down onto a stool and sigh. My feet are killing me, and I want nothing more than to run a hot bath, then soak in it for hours.

"Long day?" the bartender asks, setting a napkin in front of me.

"The longest."

I woke up this morning with an awful headache, no doubt from all the crying I did yesterday. Then when I checked my bank account—like I do every morning because I'm responsible like that—I realized somebody had made not one, not two, but *three* purchases on my card without my authorization. Guess who got to spend the morning on the phone with the bank dealing with that? Me.

Then the coffee I had delivered for room service—a splurge on its own—didn't come with cream, and when I called down to the front desk to request some, they told me they were out. Which meant I was stuck with black coffee, and I hate black coffee.

That was all before I even got out of bed.

I also had to deal with my sister freaking out about last-minute things, my mother freaking out about last-minute things, and everyone else freaking out about last-minute things. And don't even get me started on the pitying looks I've been getting from everyone who knows I just got divorced.

It has been an emotionally taxing day on so many levels.

The bartender chuckles like he's in on the joke, even though he has no idea how long of a day it really was for me. "What can I get for you?"

"Do you have chocolate milk?"

I don't know why I say it. I had every intention of getting drunk tonight, but wine doesn't sound appealing right now.

He lifts his brows, then shoots a glance down the bar. "Do we have chocolate milk tonight, boss?"

Boss?

I turned on my stool to find my least favorite person in the world right now.

Actually, probably my second least favorite person in the world right now—fuck that asshole who stole my credit card information.

I hold my breath, waiting for him to say something asinine because that's apparently the only thing that can come out of his mouth.

But to my surprise, he doesn't. He just looks at the bartender and nods. "Yeah, we do."

The bartender taps the counter twice and tells me he'll be right back, then takes off. I turn to thank him for the drink, but the words die on my tongue when I realize he's getting up and moving two stools down to sit next to me.

Like *right* next to me. So close I can smell him, and he smells divine. Almost like a hint of something woodsy with just a note of orange.

I hate that I like it.

He doesn't say anything as he takes a seat, his warmth wrapping around me like a blanket I didn't ask for. Somehow, he seems so much taller sitting beside me than he did standing next to me. I didn't think my heels gave me that much height, but I feel so small sitting beside him right now.

"You do know your sister and Collin paid for an open bar, right?"

"I'm aware."

He lifts a brow, waiting for me to elaborate. I don't because all I can hear is Thad's voice in my head. He used to get so mad at me when I would order at his work functions because it was "embarrassing."

"Chocolate milk, Hollis? Really? You're an adult—adults don't drink chocolate milk. Grow up."

But he never knew I love chocolate milk so much because it reminds me of early mornings with my father. He'd get up and have a pot of coffee and read the newspaper. He'd pour me a glass of chocolate milk and hand me the crossword section. We'd sit quietly at the kitchen table while he read and I worked.

It's always been a comfort thing for me. Whenever I'm in a high-stress situation, I have a glass of chocolate milk to calm my nerves. It helps take me back to simpler times, times when I was young and hopeful and didn't realize how cruel the world can be.

Before my husband turned out to be no better than any other man in my life and cheated on me.

"Okay," he says, and—shockingly—drops the subject. He lifts his own beverage of choice—it looks like a cocktail of some sort—and takes a healthy sip.

We sit next to each other quietly for a long time. How long, I have no idea, but it would feel too wrong to ask the guy to go away after what he just did for me with the chocolate milk.

Besides, I guess I owe him after yesterday. I try not to cringe thinking about it. That was not one of the finer moments in my life.

I have no idea what happened. My emotions got the best of me. I was already stressed heading into the situation, and he and his smug attitude didn't make it any better.

"Look, about yesterday," he says as if he can read my mind. "I'm—"

I hold my hand up, stopping him. "There's no need to apologize. I'm the one who should be saying sorry. I was completely out of line on many accounts, and I regret that. I've been going through a tough time, but I shouldn't have taken that out on you."

"I wasn't going to apologize."

I jerk my head back. "Excuse me?"

"I wasn't going to apologize. I was just going to say I'm sorry you're going through whatever it is you're going through, but I forgive you for your actions yesterday."

Oh man, this guy is rich.

"Are you serious?"

"Are *you* serious? Because as I remember it, I was doing nothing but minding my own business yesterday. *You* were the one who attacked me. Both times."

"You prodded."

"Okay, fine," he says with a shrug. "I concede to that."

"And I concede that I might have been a little…"

"Crazy? Erratic? Completely fucking batshit?"

I narrow my eyes at him, even though he's not wrong. I *was* the one who attacked yesterday—literally, even though I didn't intend to. But he's the one who provoked me. He should take the blame too.

I'm too tired to keep arguing and care though.

I blow out a long breath. "Look, it's obvious we got off on the wrong foot, and yeah, maybe I was a *little*"—I emphasize the word so he knows I'm not the only one at fault here—"crazy yesterday, but can we start over?"

He eyes me carefully, those captivating green eyes of his bouncing back and forth between my own blue ones. Watching me. Waiting. I don't know what for, but his penetrating gaze is intense enough to make me shift in my seat. I don't like how it brings me neither comfort nor discomfort.

If anything, I feel seen for the first time in a long time.

After what seems like forever, he gives me a slow nod. "Yeah, we can start over." He lifts his drink just as the bartender sets a glass of chocolate milk in front of me. "To starting over?"

"To starting over."

We clink our glasses together.

I take a sip of my chocolate milk as he downs the rest of his drink, then motions to the bartender for another.

"You didn't shrink away from me after the ceremony," he says, running a hand through his hair. "I'm impressed. And impressed that you didn't hit me or throw champagne on me."

"Well, the night is still young," I say.

"That's fair." He clears his throat and runs a hand over the five o'clock shadow on his face. "I guess I should say I'm sorry. I was a little...antagonistic myself."

"A little?"

"Okay, a lot. I'm just...I'm not really into weddings."

"Not into weddings? Don't you own this venue?"

"Co-own." He nods. "With my sister, actually. She's the one who wanted to use the extra property for weddings. I thought we should just build an activity area or open space for food trucks to come by, but she was right about the numbers for a wedding venue. It's much more lucrative than any of that."

Ah, so he's one of those guys—always about the money.

Thad was like that too. He wanted the latest and greatest, and he wanted it before anyone else could have it.

"Yes, I'm sure you're hurting for money, Mr. NHL Superstar."

"Oh, so you do know my name, then. I was starting to wonder."

I roll my eyes. "I know your name, *Lowell*."

Even though the room is dimly lit, I don't miss the way his eyes flare when I say his name for the first time, testing it on my lips and his ears.

"Cameron."

"Huh?"

"My first name—it's Cameron."

I stick my hand out toward him. "Nice to meet you, *Cameron*. I'm Hollis."

His eyes spark again as he clasps my hand. "Nice to meet you, *Hollis*."

A shiver races down my spine as my name rolls off his lips. He says it like he's cursing it and kissing it all at once.

We don't pull our hands back immediately. In fact, it's safe to say we sit there holding each other's palms for far longer than is appropriate.

I can't seem to make myself pull away, and

apparently, he can't either. I don't get it, and based on the way his brows sink lower and lower by the second, he doesn't either.

The bartender slides a new drink in front of Lowell, and we finally break the contact.

"So," I say, rubbing my hand against my thigh. I'm not sure if I'm wiping his touch off or trying to savor it. "How exactly does an NHL star who doesn't like weddings come to own a wedding venue?"

"Not just any wedding venue—a wedding venue *and* a brewery." He shrugs. "Just something fun to invest in. I don't really have much of a say around here. My sister is the real boss."

I don't know why, but I like that he doesn't take all the credit for the business as most men would. I like that he focuses the attention on his sister. Though I'm sure being an NHL player, he gets plenty of attention. He doesn't need this too.

"I suppose that makes sense, then. But if you're not into weddings, why did you give the approval?"

"Because it was what she wanted." He says it so matter of fact, and I like that too.

"I see. And you don't like weddings because…"

"And you were crying in your car yesterday because…" he challenges.

Well, shit. He has me there.

Based on the way he smiles, he knows it too. He lifts his drink to his mouth, still staring at me expectantly like

I'm going to spill my guts with just one glance. Not a chance.

"Gosh, I feel *so* much better. I had to pee throughout all those speeches. Yours was great, by the way." Emilia plops down on the stool next to me. "Oh, good, you ordered me wine."

Except I didn't order her wine. I forgot about it the moment I sat down and realized Lowell was here.

I glance around, trying to figure out who it came from, and I don't miss the way the older guy at the other end of the bar is staring intently this way, his eyes firmly on Emilia. When he finally peels his eyes from hers and realizes *I'm* looking at *him*, he flicks his gaze away.

Emilia notices none of this. She just picks up her glass, downing half of it in one go before nodding toward mine. "They have chocolate milk here?"

"I made sure they got her some."

"Oh, hey, Lowell. Didn't see you there."

"Emilia." His eyes bounce between us. "You two know one another?"

"You could say that." Emilia elbows me lightly, grinning. "We've known each other since the first grade —the first day of first grade to be exact. Hollis was really shy back then and got so nervous on the bus ride to school that she threw up in her lunch sack and didn't tell anyone about it. When lunchtime came around, I felt bad and shared half of my peanut butter and jelly with her. We've been best friends since."

I try not to react to the story because even though I

was just a kid, it's still embarrassing.

"Huh," Lowell says. "It's hard to imagine Hollis as shy."

"I can imagine it is for you. Heard she clocked you pretty good."

"Sure did. She's a fighter, that one."

"*That one* is sitting right here," I interrupt, looking pointedly at Emilia, who just smiles back at me. "Come on, let's go dance."

"But you hate dancing."

"No, I don't."

"Yes, you do. You barely even danced at your wed—" She stops midsentence, snapping her mouth shut, realizing maybe right now isn't a good time to bring that up. "You're right. You love to dance. Let's go dance." She guzzles the rest of her wine in one drink, then hops off the stool. "Besides, they're playing Queen, and you *love* Queen."

The moment she says it, my eyes find Lowell's, and his green gaze is dancing with laughter.

"Love them, huh?" he says. "Thought they were— what was it you called them again? Shitty?"

Emilia gasps. "She would never! She's *obsessed* with them."

"That so, Hollis?"

I shrug, and he shakes his head with a grin I find way too charming as Emilia drags me away.

For the first time since I met him, I'm not so sure I want to get away from him.

CHAPTER 4

I feel like a fucking creep right now.

I've been sitting at the bar for the last twenty minutes just watching Hollis and Emilia dance out on the floor. They're laughing about something—what, I don't know —but I can't help but notice that this version of Hollis is the exact opposite of the version I met yesterday.

Honestly, she's confusing as hell.

And intriguing.

I hate that she's intriguing because it makes me want to get to know her. I don't *want* to want to get to know her.

"You look like hammered dog shit."

"Thank you. I was hoping someone would notice how hard I worked to look good today."

Smith laughs, taking a seat on the stool next to me. "This have anything to do with the fight you started last night?"

"One, it wasn't a fight. Two, how do you even know about that? You weren't there."

He lifts a shoulder. "Word gets around."

"Miller?" His grin is answer enough, and I shake my head. "Fucking rookie." I toss back the rest of my cocktail and motion to the bartender for another. "It's not last night. It's just…other shit."

"Other shit like that girl you're staring at?"

My eyes drift back out toward the dance floor in the middle of the courtyard. Hollis has her arms up as she shimmies her ass from side to side. Honestly, she's a horrible dancer. Zero rhythm and doesn't know how to move her body at all.

But for some reason, I still can't look away.

"Interesting," he mutters, and I turn my attention back to him.

"What is?"

"Nothing. I just haven't seen you like this in a while."

"Like what?"

"Captivated."

I scoff. "I'm not *captivated*. I'm…"

"Interested?"

I glare at him. "Intrigued is all."

"Right."

"Dude, it's nothing."

He holds his hands up in innocence. "I didn't say it was."

"Your tone sure as shit did."

"And your insistence that it's nothing sure as shit does too."

"Because it's nothing. You know how I feel about relationships."

When everything went down with Celine several years ago, Smith was there to help me pick up the pieces and put myself back together. I was still finding my way with the Comets at the time, and Smith took me under his wing and helped me get my head screwed back on so the whole mess wouldn't affect my performance on the ice too badly. He said I was too young and had too promising of a career to let something like that get me down and get me sent back to the AHL.

So, I adopted his philosophy on life—hockey comes first no matter what. I've lived by that rule for the last several years and it's kept me on track. Because of it, I got to hoist the Stanley Cup over my head, and that's what this is all about, isn't it?

"And you get it—we have the same outlook on that," I say.

He runs a hand over his jaw, scratching at the neatly trimmed beard he keeps. "I don't know. I'm starting to think I might have been wrong about that after all."

I snap my head back, surprised by his words. "Oh man, tell me you aren't going soft on me too. It's bad enough hearing Collin and Rhodes going on and on about their wives. Don't tell me they got to you too."

He lifts a shoulder. "Nah. Just…getting older. Starting to realize the things that matter and that don't."

"Hockey matters."

"Hockey always matters. But...some things matter more."

I follow his line of sight out onto the dance floor, and unless I am completely crazy, he's looking right at Hollis' dance partner.

I have questions—*so* many questions—but much like me, Smith is a private guy. That's something we agree upon and respect about one another.

I can't help but wonder though if Emilia may just be the cause of the shift I've seen in him over the last two years. The timeline does add up...

"Ignore me," he says, interrupting my thoughts. "It's just weddings. Sometimes they get you thinking, you know? Of things you might be missing."

A sharp twinge in my chest pulls my attention.

"Missing? What could be missing?"

He gives me a look that tells me I know exactly what he's referring to, but I ignore it.

He means love. I don't miss love because I don't need it. I don't need it because I've had it and it sucks. All I need is hockey...and maybe a few one-night stands. That's it.

"Anyway." He pushes off the bar, then claps me on the back. "I'm going to go stop Miller from feeling up Ryan's grandmother. He's getting handsy, and I don't trust the rookie."

I laugh because it's probably not a bad idea. To say Miller is a bit unpredictable would be an understatement.

He turns away and takes two steps before spinning

right back around toward me. I lift a brow at him in question.

"Ask her to dance."

"Ask who to dance?"

"The girl you can't take your eyes off of. Trust me, if I could ask somebody to dance right now, I would." He glances back at the dance floor longingly before giving his head a shake and retreating into the crowd.

I peel my eyes away from his retreating back and look out at the crowd on the floor. Hollis is dancing right in the center, throwing her arms about, having the time of her life.

She looks ridiculous. Happy.

And for the briefest moment, I want to be out there with her having fun too.

The song slowly slips into a much milder tempo. Emilia motions toward the bar, but Hollis waves her off, swaying back and forth slowly by herself in the middle of the crowd.

I don't know why I do it. It could be Smith's words repeating in my head, or it could be because she looks so awkward swaying back and forth alone. Either way, I let my feet carry me forward.

I don't stop until I'm standing right in front of her. Her eyes widen, surprised to see me. I'm surprised by it too.

I don't know who makes the first move, but one second she's standing four feet away from me, and the next she's in my arms, no longer dancing awkwardly alone.

We're slowly moving around the dance floor, completely coordinated, and it feels comfortable doing this with her. Maybe it's just because I haven't been this close to someone in a long time, but her body feels good next to mine. Soft...warm.

"You're really good at this," she mutters quietly after several long silent seconds.

"Lessons."

"Huh?"

"I took dance lessons. Ballet too. A lot of hockey players do. It helps us move better on the ice, increases our flexibility and agility."

She tips her head to the side. "That is...unexpected."

"Plus, it helps us score points with the ladies."

"Is that something you need help with? Scoring points with the ladies?"

"I don't know—you tell me. How am I doing?"

"Scale of one to ten?" I nod. "I'd say a solid four."

"A four?"

"A *solid* four."

"Ah, yes, solid makes it so much better."

"I mean, it really does. You could be a soft four, which is really more like a three."

"Out of ten?"

She nods. "Afraid so."

"And how does one score a three out of ten exactly?"

She motions behind me, so I swing us around, wanting to see what she's looking at.

"You see that guy dancing with the old lady? That is a solid three. He definitely gets points for yucking it up with the elderly, but he loses a lot of points because it looks desperate, like he's trying way too hard to impress someone."

"You do know that's my teammate, right?"

"Hey, I don't make the rules, I just relay them."

"I'd say your scoring is spot-on because well, I know Miller and he is definitely trying too hard, but I'm still confused how he is a solid three while I am a solid four. I've not danced with one old lady tonight, and I certainly don't look desperate. How am I only one point ahead of him?"

"Ah, see that's where it gets kind of tricky. You haven't danced with any old ladies tonight, so you definitely lose points there. You've also not danced with anyone tonight, so you lose more points there. In fact, all you've done is sit at the bar skulking, so again, you lose more points. At that point, you're a one."

"How do you know what I've been doing all night?"

Her cheeks turn pink like she's admitted to something she shouldn't have.

"That's not the point," she mutters. "The point is the points."

"Right. And I have…one? For not being gentlemanly enough and being an antisocial asshole, but also not looking desperate?"

She shakes her head. "Four."

"How do I gain the other three?"

"Snazzy suit and scruffy sexy five o'clock shadow combined with your *lonely hearts club* attitude giving you this whole *I'm broken please fix me* vibe have brought you up a few."

"Let's definitely circle back to that snazzy suit and scruffy sexy five o'clock shadow."

"Ah, see, you spoke, so you're back down to a three. You are much cuter when you don't speak."

"Duly noted. Don't speak—got it."

"Look at that, already down to a two."

"Well, since I'm losing points by the minute, I'd like to address the whole *lonely hearts club* thing. I can assure you I am not out here looking for a lover or a friend."

"Really? This is a wedding after all. Isn't that what people do at weddings? They hook up and make one-time bad choices they'll regret later because they're sad and lonely because someone else is getting their happily ever after when they're a freshly divorced almost-thirty-year-old starting their life over."

I lift a pointed brow at her. "It sounds like you're speaking from experience there."

It would make sense though—the reason she was crying in her car, the reason she's been crying all weekend, the reason her emotions seem to be all over the place.

If she's freshly divorced, this weekend has to hurt for her.

The only indication that I might be right is the way her eyes flit away from mine just before that same sadness I saw before seeps back into her gaze, and it makes me want to hold her closer and wrap my arms around her to form a protective layer so nobody can ever hurt her again. Whoever broke her like this, I want to break them.

More than that, I want to see her happy and carefree again. I'd do anything to get that back.

I tug her closer until her body is flush against mine and drop my lips to her ear, trying not to get distracted by how good she smells when I'm standing this close to her. Her heart rate picks up at our proximity, and I can hear her breaths coming in sharper by the second.

"Tell me, Hollis, are *you* looking for a lover or friend?"

She gulps. It's so audible I hear that too.

She tips her head back, staring up at me, her tongue darting out to wet her lips. "Are you offering?"

It's my turn to be surprised because I did not expect her to say that.

"That depends... Which one are you looking for?"

She laughs, though there's no humor to it, and slowly shakes her head.

"Neither. I have no business looking for either. Not right now."

"Everyone deserves a friend, Hollis. Even you." I tip my head down until we are eye to eye. "*Especially* you."

Another stuttered breath.

Her eyes flash to my lips, then to my eyes, back to my lips once again.

47

If I were to move just an inch, our mouths would be touching. I'd be kissing Hollis, and I don't think I would be stopping anytime soon.

She opens her mouth to respond, but whatever she's about to say is cut off by a shutter sound.

I glare at the intrusion.

"Sorry," the wedding photographer says, not looking the least bit sorry at all. "You two were just... wow. The chemistry was sparking—I had to capture it."

He shakes the camera at us and snaps a few more pictures before sauntering off. The moment has passed.

I look back to Hollis, but with how stiff she's grown in my arms, I already know what's coming before she even says it.

"I have to go."

She pulls away, and I let her leave.

I don't know how long I stand there watching her walk away, and I don't know how long I stand there after she's gone.

I do know it takes me all of one second to miss her and to want to hold her again, and all of two seconds to push away the hundreds of questions already running through my head. I also know it takes me exactly thirty steps to get to the door leading outside, and it takes me one minute to find her in the gardens off to the side of the brewery.

She's sitting on a bench, her shoulders curled forward, head resting in her hands. It's obvious she's upset, but I don't know what about, and I don't know why I care so much.

Why the hell do *I care so much?*

I stalk toward her slowly and quietly, not wanting to startle her, but somehow, she knows I'm here.

"You can't be my friend, Lowell."

I take a seat on the bench next to her, not missing the tear that streaks down her face. "Why not?"

"Because I don't like you."

I laugh softly, gently reaching for her face and tipping it up so she's looking at me.

"That's fine. I don't really like you either."

It's a lie. I do like her. In fact, I can't remember the last time I liked someone as much as I like her.

I don't want to like her, just like I really don't want to be fighting this urge to press my lips to hers. I don't want to want to kiss her.

But I do.

I really, really do.

Especially when she's peering up at me with wide eyes filled with unshed tears. I want to kiss away all the sadness and all the problems she seems to be having. I want to see her smile again. I want to see her laugh.

Want to taste her.

I think she's just as surprised as I am when I press my lips to hers. It takes her a moment to respond, like she's waiting for her brain to catch on to what's happening.

I'm waiting for *my* brain to catch on to what's happening too.

Why am I kissing her? What the hell am I doing?

I don't know how long we sit like that, unmoving, our lips just resting together, but it's like all the tension snaps out of the air in a second flat and we're not sitting still anymore.

Hollis kisses me back like it's the first and last kiss she'll ever get, and I don't dare waste a second of it, sliding my hand higher into her hair, the other one going to her hip, dragging her to me until she's straddling my lap.

She lets out a low moan the moment our bodies connect, then settles against me like she's sitting right where she belongs. Her hands crash into my hair, tugging me closer and deepening the kiss.

There's no way she doesn't feel my cock through these awful dress pants, just like there's no mistaking the wet spot pressing against me where our bodies are meeting.

I drag my hands down her body, running my fingertips along her curves, memorizing them, making sure I touch every inch of her. I slip my hands over her ass and under the thin, flowy dress that's bunched around her waist. My hands slide over her cheeks, and I make a low noise of approval when I realize she's wearing a thong.

She wrenches her mouth away at the sound, her breaths coming in ragged as she stares at me with glassy eyes—this time for a reason other than tears.

"What are we doing, Lowell?"

"I'm being your friend."

She laughs softly. "I told you I don't want to be your friend. I don't like you."

"Fine. Then I'm being your lover."

She crushes her lip between her teeth. "That's a bad idea."

"I know."

"It's a really, *really* bad idea."

"I know."

"This is exactly like one of those bad ideas I was talking about earlier."

"*I know*, Hollis." I squeeze her ass cheeks, dropping my forehead to hers. "I know."

She's right. It's a really bad idea. Like the worst possible one ever.

She's my teammate's sister-in-law. Collin would kill me. Not to mention she's freshly divorced and sleeping with her right now would probably fall into a morally gray area. She's too emotionally vulnerable.

She's too—

She moves her hips, rubbing herself against my cock, which is still dying to get out of these dress pants. I grip her hips, tugging her closer because oh god does she feel good. I run my nose along her jaw, loving the smell of fresh flowers that seems to be radiating off her.

"What are you doing, Hollis?"

"I don't know."

"I thought this was a bad decision."

"It is. Such a bad one."

"The worst," I agree, peppering kisses along her neck.

She nods. "Lowell?"

"Hmm?"

She pulls back, our eyes colliding, the moon reflecting off her dark blue gaze.

If this is the moment she walks away, I want to commit it to memory. She's gorgeous, her skin slightly sticky from the heat in the air, cheeks flushed from my kisses, hair a mess from my hands.

Her mouth opens, and she says something I didn't know I needed to hear so badly.

"I want to make a one-time bad decision with you."

CHAPTER 5

HOLLIS

I haven't cried since Harper's wedding in July, a little thing I've been immensely proud of considering how stressful everything has been in my life.

But today? Today I feel like I want to cry, and it's all because I just *had* to get out of my apartment and try working somewhere else for the day.

The moment I walked into the cute little coffee shop I found a couple of weeks ago, I knew it was a bad idea. The smell in here is…ugh, it's awful today, and it's making my stomach turn like crazy. It usually smells like a sweet, delicious baked good, a big reason I come here.

Not today.

Today, the coffee smells burnt, the hazelnut syrup is making me gag, and if I have to smell one more heated-up egg sandwich, I really may hurl.

I clutch my stomach, willing myself not to puke. I just have a bit more left to finish writing, and after that I'm golden and can take the weekend *and* Monday off.

It's one of the things I love about content writing—

the flexibility. I also love being able to pick up and work anywhere I want. It made packing up my entire life and moving across the state after the divorce a whole lot easier to do.

Leaving my mother and trying to get her to understand that I was going to be just fine on my own? Well, that was a whole different story.

My stomach protests again and I press my hand against it, hoping to calm it down. I close my eyes, sucking in a few deep breaths so I don't hurl in the middle of the shop.

Come on, Hollis. Just half an hour longer. You got this.

My phone buzzes against the table, and I'm embarrassed by the way I rush to check it.

I deflate when I see it's just my mom calling for the fifth time today even though she knows I'm working. I send her call to voicemail and wait for my phone to light up with an angry two-minute-long message.

I don't know why I expected it to be anyone different. It's always just my mom calling, no matter how badly I want it to be someone else.

It's silly for many reasons. One, I never gave him my number. And two, I shouldn't *want* him to call.

I knew the score the minute I asked Lowell to take me to bed. It was a one-time thing. That was it. So me waking up disappointed by the cold spot next to me the following morning is my own fault.

Him not contacting me is probably for the best. I mean, he is my brother-in-law's teammate. Getting involved with him—again—wouldn't be the best decision. I think I'm all tapped out on bad decisions lately.

"Welcome to Cup of Joe's! What can I get you today?"

"I'll have a hazelnut latte, and then I'll take an egg—"

I reach for whatever is nearest to me—which just happens to be my laptop bag—and I lose all the contents of my stomach. I groan, wiping my mouth with the back of my hand. I reach blindly for a napkin off my table and use it to wipe my sweaty forehead.

What the hell is wrong with me?

This is the second time this week I've thrown up. First, it was from bad leftover pizza—something I never believed was a thing until I saw it splattered in the toilet. Now, judging by the noodles in the bottom of my laptop bag, it's the Chinese food I had delivered last night.

"Ugh," I grumble, tossing the napkin into the now ruined bag and sitting back against the booth I'm sitting in. "Great. Just what I needed."

"Are you all right?" someone asks from beside me.

I wave a hand, not really paying attention to them as I close my eyes and suck in a few deep, steadying breaths because my stomach is turning again.

I don't know how long I sit like that, but I'm interrupted by a sweet old voice.

"Here you are, dear." I peel my eyes open to find a

woman who looks about sixty holding a cup of water out to me. "Drink this. It'll help."

I reach for the cup and gulp it down without question. My stomach rumbles again as the water hits it, but it doesn't take long for it to settle back down.

"Thank you," I manage to choke out, my throat hurting from the puking. "And I'm sorry. I'm so embarrassed."

"It's all right, dear. We've all been there before."

"We've all puked in public before?"

"Well, most of us mothers have. It's really no big deal."

Mothers? What is she talking about?

"I'm not a mother."

"Oh, sorry. I thought…" She waves a wrinkly hand. "Well, never mind what I thought. It's not important. Do you need another glass of water?"

"Actually, that would be great, thank you. I don't think I can stand the smell of walking through the place."

She purses her lips like she wants to say something, then shakes her head, thinking better of it. She takes the cup from my hands and makes her way back up to the counter for a refill.

Mothers? I shake my head. Does the old bat think I'm pregnant? Do I *look* pregnant? I know I ate a lot of Chinese last night, but I'm not pregnant. That's not—

"Oh fuck."

"Pardon?" the old woman says, setting a new cup of water on the table.

"I…"

I have to go.

I have to go *now*.

I rise from the booth so fast water sloshes out of the cup. I don't even care that it almost hits my laptop. I'm too busy freaking the fuck out.

"Thank you so much for your help," I say to the old woman as I pack up. I toss my laptop bag into the trash, then gather up the rest of my things, slinging my purse over my shoulder. "But I have to go."

"Go? Are you sure you're in a condition to go, dear?"

No. "Yes, I'm fine. Thank you again. And sorry."

"It's fine. I'm—"

I don't hear the rest of her words.

I'm already out the door, flying down the sidewalk to the nearest drugstore. I go immediately to the family care aisle and grab no less than six kits. As a last-minute decision, I grab a bag of Solo cups and head for the bathroom.

I don't even bother paying for anything. I'll do that after. I am way too freaked out to wait around for someone to ring these up. I need to know *now*.

I rip them all open, along with the cups, and hover over the toilet, willing myself to pee.

After I dip every single stick, I wait.

And watch.

And wait.

And watch.

And wait.

And finally…I cry.

I cry because not one, not two, but all six tests say the same thing.

I'm pregnant.

"I'm preg—"

The word gets stuck in my throat, and I swallow it down.

Once. Twice.

I run my tongue over my lips and try one more time.

"I'm pregn—"

It gets stuck again.

It's the same thing that's been happening for the last three days since I took those tests. After I cried in the bathroom of the drugstore for twenty minutes, I paid for the tests and grabbed three more just to be sure, then took them home and did it all over again. The results were the same on every single one.

Just like the results were the same this morning when I heard back from my doctor.

"Congratulations, Ms. Kelly, you're pregnant."

I threw up in her office at her words. She wasn't too happy about that, or the fact that I was already nine weeks along and didn't have a clue.

After I explained that I've always had erratic periods

and have been under a lot of stress since my divorce, she understood. She asked if I was going to tell my ex-husband about the baby.

I laughed until I cried.

Then I puked again.

I still can't believe it.

How the hell did this happen?

I mean, I know *how*. I just…how?!

We used protection. I know we used protection. I literally watched him roll the condom on.

But maybe something happened. I mean, we were going at it pretty hard. Maybe it broke and neither one of us realized it. Maybe it's all my fault because I genuinely can't remember the last time I took my birth control pill because I've been too distracted by everything else going on in my life.

Maybe…

No.

I'm going to drive myself crazy thinking of all the different scenarios. None of them will change the outcome.

"I'm pregnant."

I blow out a stuttered breath, completely shocked to my core. I just got divorced three months ago, and the first guy I sleep with—completely on a whim—gets me pregnant. What the hell did I do in my past life to deserve this kind of karma?

I rest my head against my steering wheel only to jump in surprise when the horn blares. Well, if Harper didn't know I was here before, she definitely knows now.

Just seconds later, the front door opens, and she stands there, staring at me, perplexed as to why I'm just sitting in my car, beeping my horn. What she doesn't know is that I'm sitting in my car beeping my horn because I'm terrified to walk in there and tell her I'm pregnant…with Lowell's baby.

I'm mostly terrified because she has no idea we slept together.

Just then, Emilia's car pulls into Harper's driveway, and she waves excitedly at me. I don't even have the heart to wave back.

I asked Harper if we could have a girls' day today at her house. Figured I might as well let them know the consequences of my actions together rather than having to repeat it over and over again. Mostly because I'm not sure I can.

I gather my purse and my confidence and step out of my car just as Emilia exits hers.

She claps her hands. "I am so excited about today. I need a break before all those smelly stinky boys start coming back to the rink in a few weeks."

Just thinking about the rink and hockey players has me wanting to toss up my breakfast.

Or maybe that's just the morning sickness.

Either way, I hold my hand to my stomach, trying to push the feeling down. It's something I've been catching myself doing a lot over the last few days, touching my stomach.

There's a baby inside me. I'm growing human life.

It's not that I never thought I would have a baby or a family. I'd be lying if I said I didn't want those things with Thad once upon a time. In fact, I had our whole life planned out pretty much from the start.

We'd get married and it would be just us for a few years so we could navigate life as newlyweds together without the extra stress of starting a family. Then, when I turned thirty, I'd stop taking my birth control and we'd start trying. We'd have been together for eight years at that point. We'd be ready.

What I never planned on was him cheating on me and throwing everything away.

Now I'm divorced, single, and pregnant by a man that I hardly know. I have no idea how Lowell is going to react at all.

Will he be upset? Will he deny that the baby is his? Will he step up and help me raise it? Do I *want* him to help me raise a kid? Will he even want the baby?

Do I want the baby?

The moment the question crosses my mind, I know the answer.

Yes. I want this baby even if Lowell doesn't. Even if he doesn't want to be part of this child's life, I'm okay with that. I can take care of it on my own. I'm strong and independent and I—

Oh god, I'm crying again.

"Hey, hey, hey," Emilia says in a soothing voice, pulling me into her arms. "What's going on?"

"It's… It's… I-I'm…"

But the words don't come.

"Shhh. It's okay. Let's go inside and get some wine in you. That will make you feel better."

That makes me cry even harder because I can't have wine and she doesn't even know that.

We slip into the house, past Harper, who shoots me a concerned look full of so many questions. Emilia steers me to the living room and plops me down on the couch, handing me a box of tissues and a pillow as she takes a seat next to me to console me.

"I'll grab the wine," Harper says, heading for the kitchen.

"Stop!"

The word comes out harsher than expected, and she halts in her tracks.

"Stop? Is everything okay? I…" She trails off when I start shaking my head.

"No, nothing is okay."

Harper swallows thickly, then glances over at Emilia, who just shrugs.

"Can you sit?" I ask her.

She slowly lowers herself to the couch across from us. "I'm… You're… You're scaring me, Hollis. What's going on?"

I suck in several deep breaths before finally gathering the courage to meet my sister's curious gaze. When I do,

I have a feeling she already knows what I'm about to say to her.

"I'm pregnant."

Emilia gasps next to me.

But not Harper. She doesn't react.

I don't think I like that she doesn't react.

"Shut up!" Emilia says, jostling me. "You're lying."

I turn to her. "I wish I were."

"How? When? Is it"—she shudders—"Thad's?"

"No."

She blows out a relieved breath. "Oh, thank god. Dodged that bullet." The light bulb goes off for her. "Well, if it's not Thad, then who?"

I slide my eyes over to Harper.

"Lowell," she says quietly.

I swallow harshly just hearing his name.

"It is, isn't it?" Harper pushes.

When I nod, Emilia gasps again.

"W-W-What?" she sputters. "How! Where! When!"

"My wedding," Harper answers for her.

I nod again.

"*That's* where you disappeared to?" Emilia slaps at my shoulder. "You lied to me! You said you went back to your room because you weren't feeling well and thought you had come down with something."

"More like came down *on* something—some dick."

I burst into laughter at Harper's blunt words, and it's exactly what I needed. I laugh and laugh until my laughter turns to tears once again.

I don't know how long it takes me to stop crying, but when I do, there's a tissue in my hand courtesy of Emilia, and I dry my eyes.

"Sorry," I say. "I'm kind of a hormonal wreck right now."

"Don't apologize. This is kind of a life-changing situation right here."

I laugh sardonically. "You can say that again."

"What are you going to do?"

"Well, I'm sure I'll probably cry some more, but after that, I'm not sure."

Emilia laughs. "No, I mean, with the baby. Are you going to…"

"Yes," I answer her unasked question. "I'm keeping it no matter what."

She gives me a sympathetic smile because we all know my life is about to change entirely. Hell, my life already has changed entirely. Since the moment those tests in the drugstore bathroom came back positive, I've known nothing will ever be the same again.

"What happened? I thought you two weren't getting along," Emilia says.

I think back to the wedding that now seems so long ago—probably because I feel like I've lived three lifetimes over the last three days—and frown. My problems that day seem so silly compared to this.

"We weren't. Then we were. And then we *really* were." I shrug. "You know how weddings go—they make you horny and you do stupid things."

"Ha. You can say that again." She doesn't elaborate, but I'm sure it has to do with her mystery man who may or may not be a hockey player. "So, are you two like dating now?"

I shake my head. "No. It was just a one-time thing."

"He is kind of known for that." She slaps her hand over her mouth. "Sorry. Ignore that."

She has nothing to be sorry for. Based on the way he slipped out of my room so easily, I kind of figured it wasn't his first time leaving a naked woman alone in a bed.

"It's fine," I tell her, though I don't exactly feel fine. It worries me that Lowell might not take the news of the pregnancy very well.

"I, uh, hate to be the one to ask, but have you told Lowell yet?" Harper asks like she's reading my mind.

"Not yet."

"Tell him what?"

We all jump at the sudden sound of Collin's voice.

He's standing in the kitchen, staring out at us with his hands on his hips, watchful eyes darting between the three of us. He's breathing hard, one earbud still in his ear, sweaty and gross like he just got done running ten miles, and hell, he probably did.

None of us speak up, so he says, "What are you telling Lowell?"

"That he's got a nice ass!" Emilia blurts out in a panic.

It's pointless. Collin isn't stupid. He knows he just walked in on a serious conversation.

"Did he do something?"

"What? No! Well, yes, kind of."

His brows inch closer together. "I'll kill him." He spins on his heel like he's going to murder him right this instant, and I lurch from the couch.

"Stop!"

"No. If he hurt you or upset you, I'm killing him. Harper, where's our shovel?"

"It's in the garage."

"Harper!" I yell at her, rushing into the kitchen after him.

She shrugs. "Sorry, just reflex."

"Collin, stop. You can't kill him."

"And why the hell not?"

"Because I'm pregnant!"

He stops, eyes wide. "You're pregnant? What does that have to do with Lo…" It takes a moment for him to work it out, but when it clicks, his brows slam together once more. "You're pregnant and you're saying the baby is Lowell's?"

I place my hand over my belly. "Yes."

"The wedding?"

"Yes."

"I see." He nods a few times, then claps his hands together. "Well, now I'm *really* killing him."

"Collin!" Harper admonishes this time.

"What? You can't expect me to not murder him! He's

an idiot and took advantage of your sister when she was vulnerable *and* knocked her up. He needs his head smashed in for that!"

He's wrong and right.

He's wrong because Lowell didn't *take* advantage of me. Hell, I was the one who kissed him back. I was the one who told him I didn't need a friend. I was the one who asked him to make a bad decision with me.

I try not to laugh at that because this was *really* not the bad decision I was talking about. I just meant sex, a one-night stand that would make being around each other a little awkward and uncomfortable because we'd seen each other naked.

I didn't mean a *get me pregnant* kind of bad decision.

"You can't kill him yet. He doesn't even know. Let's at least see how he reacts before we commit to several years in prison." Harper tries to reason with her husband, going over to kiss him on the cheek to calm him down.

It works.

"Fine," Collin concedes. "But if that fucker so much as reacts any differently than complete and utter fucking joy, he's dead."

That doesn't sound fair at all, but I don't tell him that. I'm sure the last thing he is expecting is to hear from me, and I bet he's really not expecting what I'm going to have to tell him. If he reacts with anything other than complete shock, I'll be surprised.

I just hope he doesn't completely turn me away. I've had enough life-changing news this week.

"When are you telling him?" Collin asks.

"I, uh, was going to tell him tonight."

"Okay. That's probably best. We're about to head into preseason soon, and…" He trails off.

Right. Because Lowell is a professional hockey player.

I'm pregnant, and the father is an NHL superstar.

I did not have this on my bingo card at all.

I nod. "I know. I'll tell him."

"Good." He shakes his head, muttering something I can't quite understand, but I'm pretty sure it's nothing good about Lowell and this whole situation. He points down the hall. "I'm going to go take a shower, let you girls finish your little hormone fest." He presses a quick kiss to Harper's head, then takes off down the hall.

"Uh, hey, Collin?"

He turns back around. "Yeah?"

"Do you think I could get Lowell's number?"

He blinks once. Twice. Then drops his head, shaking it.

"So fucking dead."

CHAPTER 6

I press the decrease button on the treadmill several times, taking my speed from seven MPH to a nice brisk four MPH to cool off. I try not to burn myself out in the gym in the off-season too much, especially since I help out at summer skate camp.

Lately though, I have so much energy and pent-up frustration that if I don't do something to expend it all, I'm going to combust. I don't have a clue as to what's wrong with me, but I haven't been able to shake this feeling of irritation all summer.

I'm annoyed because I'm bored at home, but I'm annoyed when I have to leave the house. I'm annoyed when there's too much noise and annoyed when it's completely silent. Nothing feels right, everything's just slightly…off.

I'm slightly off.

I think the worst of it all is that I can almost pinpoint the exact minute I started feeling this way—the morning after Collin and Harper's wedding.

It took every ounce of willpower I had to make myself crawl out of bed and leave Hollis to sleep, but I did it because that was what we agreed upon. I did it because I knew starting something up with my teammate's sister-in-law would be really, really stupid. I did it because I was scared that I liked her a little too much, and I can't afford that.

Except ever since I left her lying there, I haven't been able to stop thinking about her.

I haven't been able to stop thinking about the way she felt under me. Or the way she tensed and whimpered just before she came. The way she moaned my name like it was a curse. And I definitely can't stop thinking about the way she tasted on my lips.

Try as I might, I can't stop thinking about her at all.

My cock starts to swell, which is really inconvenient considering I'm trying to wind down, not work myself back up.

I slow the treadmill down another notch, letting my legs cool off for a quarter mile before hitting the shower and heading home to yet another night cooped up inside my house with a Caesar salad and a Marvel movie pulled up.

Normally when I get tired of being alone, I'll call up Collin or Rhodes or even Smith. But the last two times I did, they all three shot me down, so I haven't bothered with them since.

I could call Miller and see what he's up to, but I'm

not that desperate…yet. Besides, preseason is soon. I'm sure I can find something to keep me occupied until then.

I click the machine off and grab the hand towel I have sitting in the cupholder. I run it over my face, wiping away the sweat that's dripping off me, and grab my phone.

I'm surprised to see I have a new message. I didn't hear it go off during my run, but I was pretty in the zone, so that's no real surprise.

Unknown: Hi.

That's what the first message reads, and I pinch my brows together, annoyed. I don't recognize the number, and there's not much I can discern from a two-letter word.

Then, my phone buzzes against my hand.

Unknown: Wow. That was stupid. I realize you probably have no idea who this is, huh?

And I still don't.

· · ·

Unknown: It's Hollis.

Unknown: From the wedding.

Unknown: Harper and Collin's wedding.

Unknown: I'm Harper's sister, Hollis.

I smile as she overexplains and find myself just the tiniest bit bothered that she really thinks I could possibly forget her.

I couldn't forget her if I tried, and trust me, I did.

Me: Sorry, you must have me confused with someone else. I don't remember anyone named Hollis from Harper and Collin's wedding.

Me: Wait—is that you, darlin'?

Hollis: In case you're wondering, I am hardcore glaring at you right now.

. . .

Me: Noted.

Hollis: Collin gave me your number. I hope you don't mind.

Me: I don't.

And that's the truth. I don't mind.

In fact, I'm *glad* Collin gave her my number. I can't even count the number of times I wanted to ask him for it and stopped myself from doing it.

Me: But I am surprised to be hearing from you.

Hollis: Given how we left things, I'm sure.

I'm not certain if that's a dig for how I slipped out before she woke, but it makes me feel guilty either way.

Hollis: Would you like to have dinner with me tonight?

· · ·

As surprised as I was to see her text pop up on my phone, this surprises me even more.

Do I want to have dinner with her? Yes. But I should tell her no, should tell her I'm busy or seeing someone, should remind her that the night we shared was a one-time thing.

I shouldn't be playing this dangerous game with her.

But…I want to. I really, really want to.

My fingers fly over the screen, and I hit send before I can take it all back.

Me: Yes.

I step out of my truck and toss my keys to the valet.

He looks at me like I'm insane.

"Uh, sir?"

"Put it under Lowell."

His eyes widen, recognizing the name.

"Yes, sir," he mutters, dipping his head and rushing to the driver's side of my beat-up truck that I truly have no business valet parking.

I slide a hand down my button-up shirt—something I hardly ever wear—and suck in a breath. Not that I'd ever admit it out loud, but I'm almost nervous to see Hollis.

I shouldn't be. This isn't a date or anything. It's just

dinner between two friends who have definitely seen each other naked.

But we're not friends.

Or lovers.

I have no idea what we are.

This is why this is an absolutely horrible idea. I should leave, should text her and tell her something came up.

But I can't stop myself from pulling open the door to the restaurant anyway.

It takes me all of two seconds to spot her sitting at the end of the bar. She's staring at the drink in front of her, her fingers playing with the straw, pushing the ice cubes back and forth.

God, even from the side she's more beautiful than I remember, and I remember a lot about her. Her brown hair is longer than it was a few months ago, and it's tied up in a messy, low-hanging bun that looks almost like she just threw it up and also totally intentional at the same time. She's wearing a flower-print dress paired with a cardigan over her shoulders, leaving a whole lot to the imagination.

As if she can sense my presence, she turns toward the door, and our gazes clash for the first time in months. She looks the same yet different, and I can't quite place my finger on why.

The corners of her lips tip up just slightly like she's both happy and sad to see me. I'm not quite sure how I feel about that as I make my way through the restaurant, trying to ignore the stares of the other patrons.

I don't really go out a lot, and this is a big reason why. People are always staring, talking about me behind their hands, trying to figure out where exactly they know me from, and the hockey fans who *do* know me don't always respect boundaries.

But I'm not paying attention to them right now.

The only thing I can focus on is Hollis.

We don't break eye contact. Not when I slip onto the stool next to her, and not even when the bartender stops in front of us.

"What can I get you?" they ask.

"I'll have whatever she's having."

"You got it."

I stare at her, taking her in because I can't seem to take my eyes off her.

It's not that I thought I'd never see her again. She's Harper's sister; I knew we'd be running into one another at some point. I just didn't think I'd see her again not on neutral ice.

Without thinking too much about it, I lean forward and press a quick kiss to her cheek. I don't miss her sharp inhale at the innocent gesture.

But it's not innocent. We both know that.

When I lean back, I still can't stop staring at her.

She shifts under my gaze, the smile on her lips growing shy as her cheeks turn pink. "What?" she asks, almost like she's nervous.

"Nothing. Just…it's good to see you."

She blows out a breath, taking the straw of her drink back between her fingers. "You say that now."

I tip my head in question, not understanding what she's meaning, but I don't have the option to ask because the bartender slides my drink to me, pulling us both from the moment.

"Thanks," I say to them.

"No problem. Would you like to place an order for your dinner, or did you need a moment?"

"I'm…not hungry," she says, her lips curling upward.

"Are you sure?"

She nods. "Positive. I've been…sick recently. I'm still not feeling the best."

"Not even some French fries?"

Her eyes light up when I say it. "Actually, those do sound good."

"Two orders of fries, please," I tell the bartender. "One with bacon and cheese."

Hollis lurches forward next to me, a hand covering her mouth like she's about to vomit at the mere mention of it.

I catch her by the hip to stop her from falling off the stool. "Are you okay?"

She nods, still not moving her hand from her mouth. "The ba—" Another lurch. "No bacon. *Please.*"

"Okay, yeah. No bacon." I nod at the bartender, who seems to understand what's going on, then look back at

Hollis. "Are you sure you're okay? If you're not up to this, we can get together some other time."

She shakes her head, moving her hand from her mouth and sucking in a few deep breaths. "No, I'm okay. We need to do this tonight."

"Do what tonight? It's just dinner."

She winces. "It's not just dinner though."

"O…kay." I draw the word out, completely confused by what's going on right now.

I wait for her to fill me in, but she doesn't. She turns her attention back to the drink in front of her, plunging the straw into the ice cubes that haven't melted yet.

I take a sip of my own drink and pull a face. "Ugh. What the hell is this?"

"Sparkling water."

"That is definitely not what I was expecting," I say, setting the cup down, reminding myself to ask the bartender for a real drink. "Tastes like ass."

She grins at that, then just as quickly as the smile appeared, it's gone. She's acting strange and fidgeting way too much for my liking.

Something is definitely up.

"What's going on, Hollis?"

She opens her mouth to speak, then snaps it back closed, shaking her head.

I'm starting to grow frustrated with her non-answers. I'm about to ask her just what the fuck is going on when the bartender sets the two baskets of fries between us.

Much to Hollis' horror—and mine—they forgot to leave off the bacon.

The moment the basket is on the counter, she slaps her hand over her mouth and charges toward the restrooms, knocking into not one but two waiters on her way through.

It takes me several seconds to catch up to what's happening before I take off after her to make sure she's okay. I burst into the women's restroom, not caring who else might be in there, and find her hunched over a toilet emptying her stomach.

Whatever sickness she had, she definitely still has it.

I curl my hand around hers, taking over holding her hair back for her as she continues to get it all out. When the last of her dry heaves subside, I let her go and help her to her feet. She turns into my arms, burying her face in my chest.

I just hold her.

Even when she begins to cry, I still hold her. Whatever is going on, it's breaking her…and it's breaking me to see her like this.

When her sobs die down, she pushes away from me, then wipes at her midnight eyes. Just from the look in them, I have a feeling whatever is about to come out of her mouth is going to wreck me.

"I'm pregnant."

My heart drops straight to the floor.

When she asked me to dinner, I didn't think she was asking me so she could tell me she's pregnant.

The scariest part of it all is that I know she's telling me because it involves me.

Even still, I can't help the words that leave my mouth next.

"Are you sure?"

"I'm sure. The doctor confirmed it this morning. I—"

"No," I cut her off, shaking my head. "Are you sure?"

Her eyes narrow. "You better not be asking me what I think you're asking me, Lowell."

I don't answer.

Her nostrils flare, and she shoves at my chest so hard I stumble backward out of the stall. She follows, her eyes nearly black, shaking her head as she heads to the sink.

"Am I *sure*? Are you *serious*?"

Again, I say nothing.

"Get out!" she screams, shoving at me again. "Go!"

But I don't get out. I don't go.

I can't.

I'm stuck here in this spot trying to figure out how the hell this happened.

Done with me, she throws her hands up and moves to the sink. She loads her hands up with soap and scrubs and scrubs and scrubs, all while muttering about what an ass I am.

I am an ass. I'm an ass who somehow got my one-night stand pregnant, then questioned if the baby is mine knowing full well it is.

I swallow the lump forming in my throat.

She shuts the water off, then grabs a paper towel, drying her hands.

She turns, glaring at me. "Do you have anything to say?"

"I…I don't know what you want me to say. I don't understand how this happened. I used a condom. I *always* use a condom."

She huffs out a laugh. "Yeah, well, clearly condoms aren't always foolproof."

They aren't, and they especially aren't if they've been tampered with.

I don't voice the concern, mostly because I feel sick for even thinking it. Hollis would never do that.

She tosses the paper towel in the trash, then folds her arms over her chest, watching me and waiting. I don't know what she's waiting for because I don't know what to say right now.

This isn't…this isn't how this was supposed to go.

Just one night. That's it.

Not this. Never this.

"What, Lowell? Nothing to say?"

"I don't know what you *want* me to say."

"I want you to say something other than *Are you sure* because that's about as much as you've said about the whole thing."

"I'm just…in shock right now. I haven't seen you in months and then you just show up and announce to me that you're pregnant and I'm just…trying to process it is all."

"Haven't seen me in months? *You're* the one who left *me* in bed!"

"You knew the rules," I say, and it's exactly the wrong thing to say.

She snaps her head back like I've slapped her with my words.

"Knew the rules?" She scoffs. "Yeah, I guess I did know them. But guess what, Lowell? The rules have changed. The *game* has changed. I'm pregnant whether you like it or not, and I'm having this baby whether you like it or not. If you don't want to be involved, just say so, but don't stand there and act like this is all my fault and I did it on purpose to trap you or something."

I swallow the bile that swims up my throat. She doesn't know how close she is to exactly what happened to me with Celine. Get pregnant, get married, get my money—that was the plan.

I don't know who Hollis was with before me. I don't know if she was with someone after me. And while I don't *think* Hollis would do what Celine did, there are too many variables to form an opinion right now, especially when in reality, I don't actually know her all that well.

"Oh my god." Her mouth drops open. "That's what you think, isn't it? You think I planned this, don't you? Think it was a scheme I cooked up or something." She takes a step toward me, her nose nearly touching mine.

"Well, guess what, buddy? I didn't want this, and I especially didn't want it with *you*."

She shoves past me and out of the restroom, leaving me standing there wondering just what in the fuck I'm going to do.

CHAPTER 7

"He said *what?*"

"And I quote, *Are you sure?*"

"That asshole!" Emilia bursts out, slamming her hand on the table.

"I cannot believe he'd say that." Ryan's sitting with her mouth hanging open, staring at me like I've got two heads. It's about how I felt last night when I heard it.

Harper's the only one who hasn't said a word, but I can see the way her jaw is clenched. She's equally as upset as them, and I have no doubt she's already determining how she's going to get away with his murder.

I love their outrage for me, but it pretty much went down exactly like I was expecting it to. I mean, sure, I didn't think Lowell would question whether the baby is actually his or would pretty much insinuate that I got pregnant on purpose to trap him, but I figured he wouldn't exactly be thrilled to be having a child with his one-night stand either.

God, the look on his face when I told him…there was such a mixture of emotions in such a short time. He looked terrified, which was no surprise. Then he looked like *he* might puke—again, no surprise there.

Then came the betrayal and disgust.

Those two hurt the most.

A waiter sets down a replacement basket of chips for us and drops off three margaritas. The four of us are currently sitting at a table outside a Mexican restaurant for lunch because I am a firm believer that there is nothing queso and tequila can't fix. Since I can't partake in the tequila myself, I'm leaving it to them to get drunk for me in solidarity with this hilariously bad time I'm having right now.

How did my life get so messed up in the last year?

"I hate him," Emilia says, taking a sip of her margarita, shaking her head. "He's always seemed like such a nice guy. I can't believe he'd say that."

"It's fine." I wave my hand. "It was just…shocking."

"It's not fine, Hollis," she insists. "It's far from fine. He's the one who did this to you, and he needs to step up and take responsibility for it."

"In case you forgot, I was an active participant in the whole ordeal."

"Oh, I didn't forget. I didn't forget because I am *dying* to know how the sex was, but I've been too scared to ask you because I didn't want you to burst into tears again."

I steal a chip from the basket and throw it at her.

"Hey!" She tosses one back my way, missing me completely and hitting the person at the table behind us.

They don't notice, and we all snicker at their obliviousness.

"I'm kind of curious too," Ryan says, grabbing her own chip. "Lowell has always given off this intense sort of vibe. I wonder if that carries into the bedroom too."

"I'm totally telling Rhodes you think about other dudes in the bedroom."

Ryan glares at Harper. "You wouldn't dare. He'll—actually, you know what? Go ahead and tell him. I'll take the punishment." She pops the chip in her mouth, almost giddy at that thought.

"So, how was it?" Emilia asks again.

"How was what?" I feign ignorance, taking a sip of my water.

"The sex!" She shouts it just a little too loud, drawing stares from others at the tables next to ours. "You know, the sex you had with the hot-as-hell pro-hockey player. They've got stamina for days, you know."

"Sounds like you're speaking from experience," I toss back, and she flicks her eyes away, avoiding my gaze. Dammit. One of these days, I *will* get her to talk about it.

"I'm definitely speaking from experience when I say you heard right," Ryan says.

"Can confirm," Harper agrees.

"See? I was right. Tell us."

"It was…" I lift a shoulder. "It was nice."

"Nice? *Nice?* You got pregnant from *nice* sex? How boring." Emilia pouts. "Never tell your child that."

I laugh. "I don't think I'll be telling the tale of how my baby was conceived."

"You never know. My mother told me once—in detail. Like way, way too much detail." She shudders, then reaches for her drink again. "She was drunk, which is what I'm about to be." She takes a healthy sip, then dips another chip in the queso. "Tell me or I'm going to throw this messy-as-hell chip at you."

"You wouldn't."

"Oh, I would."

She lifts it to chuck it my way, and I hold my hand up.

"Fine, fine. I'll tell you. Put the weapon down." I shake my head at her antics as she pops the chip into her mouth with a victorious grin. I glance around the table, and all of them are staring at me expectantly, apparently very invested in knowing how sex with Lowell was.

I don't know what to tell them because I don't know how to put it into words.

I don't know how to tell them I've thought about it almost nonstop since it happened. I don't know how to tell them it was the single most amazing experience of my life. How he laid me out across the bed and took his time stripping my dress from my body, then kissing every single inch of it, bringing me to orgasm twice before sliding into me and going for the hat trick. How he was gentle in the best ways and rough in all the even better ones.

And how the worst part is not even him being a giant asshole last night can taint it.

I don't know how to say any of that, so I just say, "Better than anything I've ever had before."

Not that I have much to compare it to. I've only had sex with three men in my life. One was my high school boyfriend, and that was over in about point two seconds. The other was Thad, and he was pretty much a one-trick pony…if you count just slamming into me in missionary to be a trick.

"You're totally glowing just thinking about it." Emilia grins, bouncing her brows up and down.

"I think that's just part of being pregnant."

"Or the sign of some really hot sex." She frowns like she's just remembered who that really hot sex was with. "I have half a mind to go to my uncle and tell him what a giant jerk Lowell is being. Have him mess with his equipment or something."

"While I very much appreciate it, that's not necessary."

"I could have Rhodes accidentally cup-check him during practice," Ryan offers.

I grin. "Again, thank you, but no."

"You have to know Collin is going to murder him when he hears about this, don't you?" Harper says.

"No, because you're not telling him."

"Hollis! You can't be serious!"

"I am. I'm very serious. This whole…thing…it's between me and Lowell and that's it. I don't need you ladies to deploy your men to fight my battles for me." I look pointedly at Emilia because I don't know exactly who her man is, but I don't want her getting any ideas either. "It's going to be fine. I'll figure it out."

Harper shakes her head, clearly upset with me. I'm upset with me too, especially for getting myself into this mess where the father of my baby thinks I'm just some puck bunny trying to trap him.

I have no idea what gave him the idea that that's the type of person I am, but it really bothers me that he thinks I'm even remotely capable of doing something like that. It's what kept me up half the night trying to figure it out.

Well, that and the urge to pee every damn hour.

"Have you told Mom yet?" Harper asks.

I groan. "Ugh. No, not yet. Mostly because I'm terrified she's going to start apartment hunting out here the moment she finds out."

"I'd be surprised if she already hasn't started now that we both live here."

I love my mother something fierce. She's a good person with a really good heart, and Harper and I are her entire world.

But she can also be very…suffocating. She wasn't always like that. Sure, she was a concerned mother and always wanted us girls to be careful, but it got worse after our father passed. Suddenly everywhere we went and everything we did was too dangerous. I bet if she could have gotten away with it, she would have wrapped us up in bubble wrap just to keep us from ever getting hurt again.

Keeping Harper and me safe and being overprotective is her way of coping with not just my father dying, but *how* he died—in a car accident on his way to see his mistress.

Up until that point, they'd had the perfect marriage. Sixteen years of bliss. Sixteen years of dancing in the kitchen to Frank Sinatra and lavish anniversary dinners. Sixteen years of good-morning kisses and never going to bed angry.

To say her heart broke in the worst kind of way when she discovered *why* he was out in the middle of a snowstorm would be an understatement. She wants to protect us from that same hurt.

I lay my hand over my still flat belly because, in a crazy sort of way, I kind of get it now. I haven't even met my baby yet and I already have this intense urge to protect it at all costs. I can't imagine how strong that feeling is going to be when they're nearly thirty.

"Let's talk about something else," Emilia says. "Like baby names or something. I personally think Emilia is beautiful, but I could be incredibly biased on that."

"You are," Harper tells her. "But I think we can all agree that Harper is a beautiful name too."

I look at Ryan. "Care to throw your own name in the ring too?"

"Nah. I'll keep my name to myself, thanks. Though I do think you should name your baby something badass, like Buffy or Khaleesi."

I wait for her to laugh, but she doesn't.

"Oh, what about Katniss? Or Xena? You know, like the Warrior Princess. I got it!" Emilia snaps. "Alanis! Like Morissette. She's like the crusher of men's hopes and dreams and it's amazing. Total angry-girl rock goddess."

"That is… I'll take that into consideration too."

"What if it's a boy?" Ryan points out.

"Thor. Definitely Thor," Emilia says. "No, wait! What about Thanos? Wait—no. Thor is much better."

Ryan and Emilia settle into a debate over names, but Harper doesn't join in. Instead, she slips her hand into mine and squeezes it.

"Even if Lowell doesn't come around, it's obvious that baby Buffy Khaleesi Katniss Xena Alanis is going to be so loved."

"Or Thor Thanos."

She grins. "Or Thor Thanos."

And for the first time since I took those tests, I don't feel so alone.

I was right about my mother.

I hold my phone propped on my pillow and try not to sigh as she starts listing off all the apartments she's been looking at nearby.

"And then there's one that's only about two miles up the road from you. They have a *gorgeous* garden I can picture enjoying my morning coffee in," she says, flipping the phone—like literally the entire phone, not just the camera—to show me a distorted photo of said garden.

"Looks great, Mom, but don't you think you're jumping the gun here?"

She flips the phone back around and gives me a sharp glare. "Don't take that tone with me, Hollis Pearl."

I try not to cringe at the use of my middle name, which I loathe entirely. I make a promise to myself right then to not give my child an awful middle name.

"I'm going to be a grandmother. A grandmother, Hollis! Of course I'm going to want to be part of that child's life, and I can't really do that from the other side of the state, now can I?"

I want to point out that yes, she can, and I will make trips back and forth all the time, but I know no matter what I say, it won't be enough. I may as well resign myself to the fact that my mother *will* be moving out this way with or without my approval. It's only a matter of time now.

"I know, Mom, I just—" My words are cut off by a big yawn, and a frown tugs at her lips the moment my mouth opens.

"What's wrong? Everything okay?"

I barely resist the urge to roll my eyes. "Everything's fine. I'm just tired, you know. Growing life and all that. I'm sure you remember what that's like."

"Oh, gosh, do I ever. You girls wore me out so badly before you were even born. Especially Harper because she was just so unpredictable." A sweet smile tugs at her lips. "Forever marching to the beat of her own drum, that one."

She's right. Harper's always been just who she is and has never apologized for it a day in her life. I've always admired that about her and wish I could say I've done the same, but I haven't. Where Harper has always been the type to stand out in a crowd and try new things, I've been the type to blend in and not take many risks. It was easier that way. Safer.

Of course the one time I step out of my comfort zone and do something risky, I get punished for it.

I pat my stomach. *Sorry, little bit, you're not a punishment.*

"Anyway, I should let you get some rest," my mother says, surprising me. "I'm sure this week has been very exciting for you."

Exciting isn't the exact word I'd use for it.

When I told her I'm pregnant, the first thing she asked was if the baby is Thad's and if we'd be getting back together. At first, I was really hurt that she thought I'd go back to him after what he did to me. But when she blew out a relieved breath when I told her not a chance, I was glad.

She asked if I was dating someone, and I said no.

After that, she dropped it. I was surprised she didn't press the issue and ask more questions since she's typically all up in my business about everything else. I think she could sense my turmoil regarding the situation. She's not asking now, but I know she will later, and I'm already dreading the conversation.

"Something like that," I murmur.

Concern pulls at her eyes and I can tell she has so much to say, but she doesn't say it. Instead, she says, "I love you, Hollis. Everything will be okay."

And because I'm a complete hot mess, tears sting my eyes. This week has been exhausting, and I don't think I realized how badly I needed to hear that from my own mother.

"Thanks, Mom. I love you too."

"I know." She winks. "Get some rest, okay? Call me tomorrow."

"I will. Good night."

"Good night, kiddo."

I toss my phone onto the pillow beside me and roll over onto my back. I stare up at the ceiling, running my hands over my stomach, marveling at the fact that I have a little cherry-sized human growing inside of me.

Harper was right. Even if Lowell doesn't come around, I know this baby will be loved and cared for. I have support from some of the greatest people in the world who will make sure that holds true.

"Everything will be okay," I tell myself as my eyes drift shut.

This time when I say it, I almost believe it.

CHAPTER 8

"Hold your horses! I'm coming!"

I push my arm through my shirt as I amble through the house to find out who the fuck is knocking on my door at this hour. It's barely seven AM, and I have no clue who it could be. Only three people on the team even know where I live—and one of those people is Coach.

Blurry-eyed, I bump into a table in the hallway.

"Fuck," I mutter, annoyed at the table and myself. I've slept like absolute dog shit last two nights, and I'd really rather not deal with whoever is standing on my porch right now.

I yank the door open, a scowl firmly in place. "Wh —" I don't even get the full word out before a fist connects with my face and I stumble backward into the house. "What the…" I clutch my face as Collin shoves his way inside my home.

He slams the door behind him, then slams me into the wall so hard I'm going to be surprised if there's not a dent in it. He drags his forearm over my throat, holding me in place as he gives me a murderous glare.

"What the hell, man?" I spit out, and he doesn't even flinch when my blood splatters against his face. "What the fuck are you doing in my house, Wright?"

"What the hell is wrong with you?" he hisses, shoving into my windpipe with just enough pressure to knock the breath out of me. "Huh? What in the actual fuck is wrong with you, Lowell?"

He shoves his arm into my throat again, this time hard enough that I choke. I make a halfhearted attempt to try to fight him off, but the prick is big and not going anywhere. Besides, I know deep in my gut that I deserve this and so much more.

I was a total dick to Hollis the other night. The second the shock of everything wore off, I knew I was completely in the wrong.

She wouldn't be setting me up. I know she wouldn't. We didn't spend a lot of time together, but I *know* she's not that kind of person.

After she told me, I was up half the night staring at my phone trying to decide whether I should call or text and what the fuck I was going to say to make everything better. I kept coming up blank because I have no idea how I *am* going to make it better.

Shit. It's been thirty-six hours and I *still* don't know how I'm going to make it better.

"I…I'm sorry, okay? I fucked up. Are you happy?"

His eyes narrow on me, making sure I'm telling the

truth. Satisfied with what he sees, he shoves on me once more before releasing me, letting me drop back down to my feet.

I gulp in deep breaths of air and wipe at the blood leaking from my nose and mouth.

"Shit, man," I say, still trying to catch my breath. "You're lucky I've already lost my real teeth or else I'd be really pissed."

"Yeah, well, join the club because I *am* pissed." He shakes his head at me. "What the fuck, dude?"

I take a few more deep breaths before pushing off the wall and righting myself. I shove past him, making sure to knock him in the shoulder, and head for the kitchen to clean off all the blood and get an ice pack.

He follows behind me, no doubt glaring holes into the back of my head.

"Did you really ask her if she's sure it's yours?"

I grimace at his words as I pull a bottle of water from the fridge and twist off the cap. I swish the water around my mouth a few times to get the taste of blood out. Then I down the rest of it in one drink and close the fridge, not bothering to offer Collin anything because screw him after what he just did.

I mean, I deserved it, but screw him.

"I…sort of implied," I finally say after several long moments.

"And did you also *imply* that she got pregnant on purpose to try to trap you?"

Another grimace, which is answer enough.

I grab the dish towel that's hanging off the stove, run it under some cold water, and press it to my split lip that's no doubt doubled in size already.

Fuck, Collin hits hard.

"I have to ask again...what the hell is wrong with you, Lowell? Why the hell would you say that to her? Do you really think that is something Hollis is capable of?"

"No! Not at all."

"Then why did you say it?"

I narrow my eyes at him. "You know why."

"Because of that shit with Celine all those years ago?"

"Yes!"

"Dude!" He runs his hands through his hair like he's irritated with me. Well, I'm fucking irritated with him, barging into my house and hitting me at the crack of dawn. "Get the fuck over it already."

"It's not exactly that easy."

"Yes, it is. Because they are two completely different people."

"You think I don't know that?"

He holds his arms wide. "Apparently not, because here we are."

"I freaked, okay? In my defense, I had just found out my one-night stand got pregnant. Kind of a lot to take in, no?"

He grinds his teeth together. "I owe you another for that too—for taking advantage of her when she was vulnerable."

"It wasn't like that," I argue, because it wasn't.

At least I don't think it was.

Fuck…was it? Did… Did Hollis not want it too? I knew she was struggling with the wedding and how fresh her divorce was, but it's not like I pressured her into anything. Hell, she was the one who asked me to make a bad decision with her. Did I do something wrong by saying yes?

"How did that even happen? Did you not wrap your shit up?"

"Of course I did! I just… The condom was kind of old, all right? It was one I'd had in my wallet for a while."

"A while? How long is a while?"

I screw my face up, not wanting to admit it. "A…year. Or more."

He tosses his head back with a groan. "Holy fuck. No wonder you got her knocked up."

"Hey, it's not like I went to your wedding in hopes of falling into some pussy, okay? That wasn't part of my plan at all. I know how desperate unattached women at weddings are to attach themselves to someone. I was not about to get mixed up in that."

"But you did. You did get mixed up in it, and look where that got you."

Fuck. He has me there.

I rest my elbows on the counter and drop my head into my hands. I can't believe I got myself into this situation. Again, technically.

Only this time, it's real. It's very real and very fucking scary.

"How are you feeling?"

"Like shit. My face hurts, and I now have a pounding headache and I think my tooth is loose. And I'm—"

"No, not that. About the baby, you idiot."

Right. That.

That is a whole different barrage of emotions I'm not sure I want to get into this early.

I'm scared.

I'm angry.

I'm worried.

I'm confused.

I'm so many different things, and I'm having a really hard time processing it all.

"I—"

Another loud knock sounds on the door, interrupting me.

Who the hell is it this time?

I look to Collin, and he shrugs. "Beats me."

I push off the counter and head for the front door. I peel it open, and, for the second time this morning, a fist connects with my face.

"Ow! Son of a bitch!" I cradle my nose, which is now bleeding along with my lip as I stumble back from the impact.

"You stupid fuck!" Rhodes rages, tossing me against the wall just like Collin did. "Are you insane? Do you have a death wish? Do you—"

Movement from down the hall catches his attention. Collin's leaning against the wall, arms crossed, clearly enjoying the show.

"Don't mind me," he says. "Please continue."

I shove at Rhodes, trying to get the beast of a man off me. He glares up at me, shoving me into the wall once more before letting me go.

I can't decide if I want to keep my nose covered or rub at the bruise that is no doubt forming on my chest at this point.

"Fuck," I mutter, looking between them. "Is anyone else going to punch their way into my house today?"

The door, which was never closed, is pushed open, and in steps Miller.

"I won't hit you, Lowell." He holds his hands up. "I can't afford to mess up these silky mitts."

"Why the hell are you all here so early?"

"Uh, because apparently you're a dumbass who needed an ass beating, and that's saying something coming from me," Miller explains. He shuts the front door, then claps his hands. "So, what's for breakfast, boys? I'm starving."

With a sigh, I shake my head and leave them in the hallway while I head to my bedroom for a clean shirt since this one now has bloodstains on it after I got punched in the face twice.

How is it not even eight AM and I've already been bloodied and bruised?

After I grab a shirt, I head back to the kitchen. Collin

and Rhodes are leaning against the island glaring at me. Miller is helping himself to a pot of coffee but can't seem to figure out how the filter works.

I shove him out of the way and finish the job, setting the sizing for a full pot and pressing start before turning around to meet the glares of my teammates.

"Harper?" I point at Collin.

He nods.

"Ryan?" I say to Rhodes.

Another nod.

I look at Miller. "Then why the fuck are you here?"

He shrugs. "I was just coming over because I was bored and the summer skate camp isn't for another few hours. I honestly have no idea what's going on."

"It's like seven in the morning!"

"Are you really going to be mad at a guy for missing his captain?" He juts out his lip, pouting in a way that makes me want to be the third guy to throw a punch today.

Instead, I just roll my eyes at him and turn to grab the now-finished coffee. I grab two mugs—because fuck Collin *and* Rhodes—from the cabinet above the pot, pour a cup for me and a cup for Miller, and slide one his way.

"Thanks," he says, taking a loud sip. "So, what'd I miss?"

His innocence makes us all chuckle.

"Dipshit over here"—Rhodes hitches his thumb my way—"slept with Harper's sister at the wedding."

"You dirty dog, you." Miller smirks at me, shaking his head. "Thought she was too crazy for you?"

I don't answer him. The only person who is crazy at this point is me for thinking what we did was a good idea.

"That's not all," Collin adds. "She's pregnant."

Miller gasps. "No way! Did you not wrap it?"

I toss my head back on a groan. "Why does everyone keep asking me that? Of course I did!"

"Not well enough, apparently. You gotta double up and shit."

Rhodes shoots Miller a concerned look. "You do *not* double up. Ever. Do you do that?"

"Uh…n-no," Miller says, not sounding the least bit convincing.

I'm not even touching that right now. I don't have the energy. I have my own problems to be dealing with.

"What are you going to do?" Miller asks the million-dollar question they are all wanting an answer for.

Fuck. What *am* I going to do? I wasn't looking for this and certainly wasn't prepared. Hell, I went to dinner with Hollis half-expecting to get my dick wet at the end of the evening. I didn't expect this major, life-changing bomb to be dropped on me.

So, what am I going to do?

Long term? I don't have a clue. That's not entirely up to me.

But I know what I need to do short term, and that's apologize to Hollis…if she'll let me.

I look at Collin and Rhodes, who are both staring at me, waiting to hear what I have to say. I swallow the lump that's been hanging out in my throat since yesterday, then blow out a heavy breath.

"I guess I have a phone call to make."

CHAPTER 9

HOLLIS

After we left things at the restaurant the other night, the last thing I expected this morning was to receive a call from Lowell asking if he could come over.

I told him no at first because I wasn't sure if I wanted to deal with the stress of seeing him before my appointment this afternoon, but he insisted on it and eventually I caved. Which is why I'm currently standing in front of my mirror in my third outfit of the morning trying to talk myself out of changing again.

Part of my brain is screaming that I should wear that leather mini skirt I bought two months ago because pretty soon I'm going to be too big to even get it up past my hips, but I know that's completely impractical.

If it wasn't for nausea and headaches and hormonal changes, you wouldn't know I was pregnant. Everything looks the same, though I know that's not going to be the case in the coming months.

I don't know how I feel about that yet, seeing my body change like it's going to. I know some women love being pregnant and love the way their bodies look while others loathe it. I wonder where I'll fall on the spectrum.

I tuck two rolled-up pairs of socks into my bra, then grab a pillow off my bed and stuff it under my shirt. I check myself out in the mirror, trying to imagine what I'll look like waddling around with a little human inside of me.

It'll be…different, that's for sure. I'm going to look like a whole different person. Hell, I'm going to *be* a whole different person. That's hard to reconcile sometimes.

A knock sounds at the door, pulling me from my thoughts.

Shit! Lowell.

My heart rate picks up and my palms start to feel sticky. It's stupid. I shouldn't feel this way about the man whose baby I'm carrying, but I do.

I'm nervous because *he* makes me nervous.

I'm nervous because I have no idea how this conversation is going to go.

I'm just…nervous.

I pull the pillow from my stomach and toss it to the bed before darting for the front door. I take a deep, calming breath, brushing a hand through my hair. When I feel like I'm not going to pass out, I pull it open.

Collecting my breath was a smart move because the moment my eyes land on Lowell, he steals it back. He's just so…magnetic. I don't want to be drawn to him. I don't want him to be north and me to be south.

He's wearing a simple light gray shirt and a pair of jeans that hug his thighs just a little too well. There's a baseball cap slung backward on his head, and he's sporting what looks like a fresh cut on his lip that I want to ask him about.

When I reach those green eyes that make me feel all kinds of things I don't understand, I find that he's looking at me with a searching gaze, like he's looking for any indication I'm going to slam the door in his face.

I won't…yet.

Instead, I move aside, allowing him to pass. The moment he steps over the threshold, I breathe again.

I close the door behind him, leaning against it because all of a sudden I'm feeling lightheaded. I don't know if it's from being close to him or just being plain exhausted, something I am more than not lately.

He looks around the small apartment, and I realize then this place must be laughable compared to wherever he lives. He's a freaking hockey player. He probably has a mansion…or two.

When he's done with his perusing, he shoves his hands into the pockets of his jeans and looks at me. His eyes do a slow scroll of my body, starting at my feet, going all the way up. He inspects me closely, not missing a single inch, like he's looking for any sign that I truly am pregnant. I want to tell him I'm not showing yet, but before I can get the words out, he grins.

"Well, those grew a lot faster than I expected."

My brows pinch together, and I look down.

Oh god.

My cheeks are on fire as I reach into my bra, pluck the rolled-up socks out, and toss them onto the couch.

"I was…practicing."

"Having tits?"

I glare at him, pushing off the door and heading into the kitchen. "Would you like something to drink?"

"Uh, yeah. Vodka if you got it." I send him a look, and he laughs. "I was kidding. Though a drink does sound good right now. I'm, uh, kind of nervous."

"You? Mr. NHL Superstar, nervous?"

He grins at the nickname as he takes a seat at the little breakfast nook. "Hockey players do get nervous, you know."

"Huh. Would have figured you'd be used to the pressure by now."

"This kind of pressure is a bit different."

"That's fair." I pull open the fridge and reach for the container of orange juice. "I don't have vodka, but I have mixer."

"Mixer works too."

I grab two glasses from the cabinet and pour each of us a cup. It's funny because I've never been a huge orange juice person, but for some reason, it's almost all I want to drink these days.

I slide a glass Lowell's way, then return the juice to the fridge before grabbing my own glass and leaning back against the counter.

"Should you be standing?"

My eyes fall to slits. "Fair warning, there are many sharp objects in this kitchen I can stab you with."

"I will take that into consideration." He smirks at me over the rim of his orange juice before taking a sip, wincing at the sting of the acidity on the cut in his lip.

"What happened to your face?" I ask.

"Collin."

I lift my brows, surprised.

"And Rhodes," he adds.

"Because of…?"

He shifts uncomfortably on the stool, not meeting my eyes when he says, "You."

Ah. So *that's* why he called me up—because Collin and Rhodes made him, not because *he* actually cares.

"They aren't why I called, though," he says like he knew exactly what I was thinking. "I was going to call before they…well…" He motions to his face, then clears his throat. "I just didn't really know what to say."

"And now you do?"

"No." He laughs humorlessly. "Not a damn clue, but I couldn't just sit by and let you think bad thoughts about me either."

"I wasn't thinking bad thoughts about you."

It's not a total lie.

Did I think he was a dick for questioning the legitimacy of my accidental pregnancy? Most definitely. But…I also understood. Given the way we met, I'm not entirely sure I can blame him for lashing out during an emotional moment.

He lifts his cap off his head, then scrubs a hand through his deep brown hair before replacing it. He sighs. "I, uh, was engaged before."

My brows shoot up because this is very much news to me, especially given how much he protested weddings.

"It was several years ago. I was seeing this girl for about eight months, and it was pretty serious, you know." He shrugs. "I loved her."

He chugs the rest of his orange juice, then gets up and heads for the sink. He rinses the glass out, sticks it in the dishwasher. I watch him move around my kitchen as if he lives here too, and I'm not sure how I feel about the fact that I don't exactly hate it.

When he's finished, he turns to me, resting his back against the counter opposite me. He crosses his arms over his chest, and I do my best to ignore the way his shirt stretches over his muscles as he stares a hole into the floor.

"I proposed when she got pregnant."

My eyes snap to him, surprised.

Is he…already a father?

"We made the engagement announcement, planned the wedding…the whole thing. I was happy. I was excited. I wanted the wife and the baby and future. Four months." His lips pull tight, and he shakes his head once before finally looking me in the eye. "It took me four months to learn she was lying."

The pain in his eyes is so clear, and I have the urge to cross the kitchen and wrap my arms around him.

Whoever this woman is, she did a number on him, and it really makes me hate her for hurting him.

"She was never pregnant. She just wanted me to propose and shotgun the wedding so I couldn't back out. And I bought it, you know? I was so young and stupid and in love that I bought it. I didn't question a thing. All of her doctor's appointments were on days I had games, and I never once thought to question it because who actually thinks the person they love is out to screw them over like that?"

He stares at me but not really at me. It's more like he's staring through me, like he's back there in the past and hearing all over again that she lied to him.

He looks so…broken.

"I'm sorry that happened to you," I say quietly, and he snaps out of whatever haze he's in.

He sniffles a few times, then shakes himself off like he's shaking off the memories.

"It's why I assumed the worst about you—because I've been there before—but I shouldn't have done that. I shouldn't have put my past on you like that. *I'm* the one who's sorry."

I nod. "Thank you for telling me."

"Thank you for not lying." He narrows his eyes. "Right?"

"I'd say my morning sickness the other night was a pretty good indication that no, I am not lying."

He nods a few times. "For what it's worth, I'm sorry you're in this situation."

"I'm sorry, too. I definitely did *not* plan this."

He gives a halfhearted chuckle. "I definitely didn't either."

I finish off the rest of my orange juice, and he takes the cup from me, rinsing it and placing it in the dishwasher as well. I'm struck again by how comfortable he seems to be in my apartment and how much it doesn't bother me. Normally if somebody came over here and started acting like this was their place too, I'd be annoyed, but—and maybe it's because I'm carrying his baby—I don't feel that way with Lowell.

"How are you feeling?" he asks.

"Tired, nauseous. Like I have to pee a lot. I keep having weird dreams of blonde babies who are babies but also look like old people." I shudder. "It's weird."

I don't tell him the other recurring dream I've been having because it's about him. I keep dreaming that he offers to pay me a million dollars to take my baby and leave, to never contact him and to never, ever breathe a word of it to anyone. It's had me waking up crying the last two nights, but I keep that to myself.

He laughs. "And about the baby? How are you feeling about that?"

"Scared," I say honestly. "Like really, really scared. But also…okay." He nods like he understands. "And you? How do you feel…about the baby?"

"Scared. Like really, really scared," he echoes.

I smile because it comforts me that he's also terrified by this new adventure we got ourselves into.

"When did you find out?"

"Officially? On Monday. Unofficially? Last Friday."

"How?"

"Hazelnut lattes and egg sandwiches."

He tips his head, brows drawn together. "Hazelnut lattes and egg sandwiches?"

"Yep. I was sitting at Cup of Joe's, and the smell of those two things was so overwhelming that I vomited in my laptop bag. Honestly, if it weren't for the old lady who commented on it, I wouldn't have thought twice, and I still might not even know today. My period hasn't been normal for a while because of all the stress with the divorce and everything, and since we used protection, I never even suspected I might be pregnant."

I feel kind of stupid for not being more in tune with my body or questioning why I hadn't had a period in months, but there's nothing I can do about that now.

My phone buzzes against the counter, and I know what it is before I even look. I cross the kitchen to check it and can feel Lowell's eyes on me the entire time.

"Did you need to take that?" he asks.

I shake my head. "It's not a phone call, it's an alarm. I have an appointment."

"For the baby?"

I nod. "Yep."

"And you're going now?" I nod again. He pushes off the counter. "I'm coming with you."

"You don't have to."

"You're right. I don't *have* to—I *want* to."

113

"You...*want* to be part of this?"

He scowls more deeply than I've ever seen him scowl before. "You're fucking kidding me, right? Of course I want to be part of this. Why wouldn't I want to be?"

I shrug. "I don't know. We don't really know each other all that well. I mean, yeah, we had this connection and shared a night together, but that's it. It's not like either of us planned to continue seeing each other past that one night. This...this is different than just bumping into one another after having sex and doing the whole *We've seen one another nude* awkward dance thing."

"I remember."

"This isn't something we just walk away from in the morning, Lowell."

"I know."

"This is a baby. This is *forever*."

He growls. "I know what it means, Hollis, and I want it."

"Are you sure?"

"Surer than I've ever been in my entire life."

I try not to let my relief show. As much as I was prepared for the opposite, I was hoping he'd say that.

"Okay. Then we should probably go. My appointment is in an hour."

"Remind me again why we got here thirty minutes early when our appointment was twenty minutes ago and we're still waiting?"

Our appointment.

I don't miss that he says that. The way he's inserted himself into this makes my stomach flutter, and I don't know if that's a good thing or bad thing yet.

He drove the exact speed limit on the way here, which drove me nuts. Then he wouldn't let me out of the truck unless he opened the door, which was also annoying, albeit a little cute.

He insisted on helping me down and carrying my purse. I really wanted to remind him that I'm barely even pregnant and he was being extremely extra, but every time I opened my mouth to say something, I couldn't get the words out. I think it's because I'm just relieved he wants to be part of this with me.

I don't have any crazy notions that we're suddenly going to be dating and then get married and live happily ever after. That's not going to happen, and I'm fine with it. But just the fact that he's here? That he's not running away or trying to toss money at me to keep quiet about the baby?

Yeah, it makes my stomach flutter for sure.

"I'm sure it'll just be a few more minutes."

He shoots me a look that says that's not likely. "We've been here forever."

"I know, but what can we do about it?"

He huffs, then before I know it, he's marching across the room.

"Lowell!" I whisper-yell at him, and he ignores me. "*Cameron!*" I hiss.

This time he turns around, his eyes sparking at the use of his first name before he holds his hand up like he's trying to calm me. He saunters up to the front desk with just enough cockiness, the kind that isn't *so* much that it makes him look douchey. He rests his forearms—the forearms I *know* look incredible—on the counter and leans across it toward the young nurse sitting there.

"Hey there," he says to her, using that same voice I've heard from him before—slick and silky and all kinds of hot. "I was wondering if you could tell me about how much longer it's going to be, *Josie*."

He puts extra emphasis on her name, laying the charm on thick.

And it works. Red steals up her cheeks, and she bats her lashes up at him.

"Let me just check really quick. What's the name again?"

"*Lowell.*" Again, more emphasis on the name. "Was kind of hoping we could get in soon. I have *hockey* practice in a bit, and…" He trails off, waiting for her to connect the dots.

If the way her eyes sparkle is any indication, she knows just who he is, and I have a feeling we're about to be next. She turns to the computer, her fingers flying over the keyboard, her mouse clicking rapidly.

And then… "Ah, you're in luck. The doctor will see you now."

"Really? Wow. Thank you *so* much, *Josie*."

He sends her that same panty-melting smile he gave me at Harper's wedding, and I'd bet a hundred dollars that girl's chair is wet right now.

Lowell waves me over as she rises to buzz us in.

I lift my brows at him. "You're incorrigible, you know that?"

"I have no idea what you're talking about," he says, holding the door open for me. "Now let's go see our baby."

Our baby.

I don't miss that he says it.

And I don't miss the way it makes me feel.

CHAPTER 10

"I brought donuts."

I hold up the baby blue box of this city's best-kept secret as a peace offering for being a few minutes late.

Hollis looks surprised to see me. "You're here."

"Yes?" I don't know why it's a question, but I also don't know why she's questioning my presence. "We have an appointment, right?"

"I wasn't sure you wanted to go since I haven't seen you in a while…"

"As long as it doesn't interfere with hockey, then I'll be there. Always."

I won't lie and say I haven't been avoiding her a little but that's because I don't know *how* to be around her. Does she just want me hanging out over at her place? Does she want to come to mine? Are we supposed to be spending time together at all? I don't really know how to navigate this. I've never had to before.

In fact, I haven't spent time with someone I've slept

with since Celine, and everyone knows how that turned out.

Hollis shakes her head. "You know what, never mind. It doesn't matter. We should get going. We're late."

"I know, and I'm sorry about that," I say as she shoves out of her apartment, then turns to lock it. "Which is why I brought donuts to make up for it."

"You're late, so you decided to make yourself *more* late by stopping to pick up donuts?"

"Well, no. I had the thought to get donuts first, and when I was leaving with the donuts in hand—completely on time, mind you—my truck wouldn't start."

She shoots me a look as we step into the elevator and she presses the *Lobby* button. "Let me put on my shocked face that your POS truck wouldn't start. Tell me, Lowell, just exactly how many layers of duct tape are holding up your bumper?"

"Hey! I'll have you know Fiona takes great exception to being talked about that way."

"Fiona? You named your truck Fiona?"

"Yep. *Princess* Fiona to be more accurate. Like from *Shrek*."

It takes her a moment to get it. "Because she's big and green and ugly."

"Precisely." I grin as we step out of the elevator. "Anyway, it's not her fault," I say, holding the door to her building open for her, trying to score some points back. "It was mine. I knew better than to risk turning her off. She gets kind of pissy when it's cold out."

"I am so confused about why you're driving around in that hunk of junk. Don't you make like six and a half million a year?"

"First, it's seven. Second, don't you dare call my baby a hunk of junk. She has feelings, you know."

Hollis rolls her eyes as I open her car door for her. "Need I remind you"—she climbs into the truck, then points to her belly—"you'll have a baby to worry about soon too."

"I'll get a second car, then. I'm not giving Fiona up yet though. I can't. Here." I hand her the donuts and make sure she's safely in the vehicle before closing the door and heading to my side. I climb behind the wheel of my beloved albeit beat-up truck and crank the engine.

Just like at the donut truck, she fusses about it. It takes three tries, but she eventually fires, and we're pulling out on the road.

I can feel Hollis' stare on me, and I glance over at her. "What?"

"Nothing."

"Not nothing. What?"

She waves her hand toward the dashboard with an amused grin as if that explains everything.

"What? It's part of her charm," I explain. "Besides, she can't go until I'm done playing hockey."

"And how close are you to being done?"

"Like ten years if I'm lucky."

"I don't think this truck can last ten more years."

"Shh! Stop jinxing it!"

She snorts, then flips open the box of donuts. She plucks one out and holds it up as if to ask me what kind.

"Boston cream."

She nods, then takes a huge bite, and I nearly swerve off the road when a bit of white cream dribbles down her chin. She wipes it away quickly before I do something stupid like park this truck and haul her into my lap and remind us just how we got into this situation in the first place.

"What's your big attachment to her anyway?"

Big attachment to...?

Oh, right—my truck.

I try to adjust myself as inconspicuously as possible and shrug. "I don't know. She's just... Well, she's been there with me through it all. Got her when I was sixteen. Paid for her myself after working and saving for two years." I pat the dash lovingly. "We've been through high school, college, the draft, the NHL...everything."

We pull up to a stoplight and I glance over to find Hollis' lips pulled into a smile. "Is she your lucky charm, Lowell?"

"What? No." I feel the tips of my ears heat at my lie. "I don't believe in lucky charms."

"Pretty sure being superstitious is like rule number one for playing hockey."

"Oh yeah? You a hockey expert now?"

She wrinkles her nose. "Nah. I'm actually not really into it."

"You're... Excuse me?"

"Yeah, it's just not really my thing."

"I… Wow. I'm speechless right now."

"Sorry?"

"It's okay. I think. Maybe." I slap my hand against the steering wheel. "No, no. It's not okay actually. Like… how? *How?* Hockey is…"

"Eh."

"Eh? *Eh?*" I shake my head. "I'm going to make you love it. Just watch."

"You can try, but I doubt it."

"That's what your sister said too, now look at her. I'm pretty sure she painted her face for at least half of the games last season."

"That's because she's insane."

"And you're not?"

"No."

"Hmm. I seem to recall a certain someone punching a certain someone else over their music being too loud. I'm pretty sure that qualifies as insane."

"Not if it was justified."

I shake my head with a grin and focus on the road. The drive to the doctor's isn't far, and we're pulling into the parking lot in no time. She was worried about being late, but we're still thirty minutes early.

I shut the truck off and look over, just watching her as she stares out the window. Her lips are slightly parted and there's a little wrinkle between her brows with how deep in thought she is right now.

I want to reach over and run my finger over all the

lines marring her forehead, brush them away along with all her worries and doubts. But I'm scared if I touch her, I won't be able to stop.

"You okay?" I ask quietly.

She jumps slightly, almost like she forgot I was even here, then clears her throat. "Yeah. I just… Sorry. Got lost in thought for a minute."

"What are you thinking about?"

"Honestly? Everything. How good these donuts taste. The appointment. How we're going to raise a child together when you're a professional hockey player and away half the year. How our whole lives are changing. Just…everything." She sighs, then tosses the half-eaten donut into the box, looking exhausted by the day already.

I get it. It's a lot to take in.

"We don't have to think about all that now. We have time still. I think right now, we just need to focus on getting to know each other better."

She snorts. "Right. Because we don't really know each other beyond the bedroom, do we?"

"I personally think the bedroom is a really good place to know someone."

"Yes, I am well aware of that fact about you."

She smiles, but it's sad, and that makes *me* sad. I know she's worried about so many things—and I am too—but I don't want today to be about all the stress of what's to come.

"Tell me about the appointment today," I say to distract her. "What's going on?"

"We get to hear the baby's heartbeat."

I sit up straight. "We do?" She nods. "Is that why you're nervous?"

Another nod. "Yes. I'm just…scared. Worried."

"About what?"

"That we won't hear anything."

Screw my rule about not touching her. I need to touch her right now. I reach over and grab Hollis' hand, lacing our fingers together. She's surprised by it at first, but it doesn't take her long to relax. Her shoulders drop as she sags against the seat like just my touching her has somehow taken some weight off her shoulders.

It makes me feel bad because it didn't even cross my mind that something like that was a possibility. The thought of that happening makes me sadder than I thought possible, and I'm surprised by that.

When everything happened with Celine, I put up walls. A lot of walls—like *all* the walls when it came to anything serious. No relationships. No promises of futures. Not even breakfast the morning after because it just set too many expectations and I wasn't in the business of fulfilling them.

Since I met Hollis, I've felt the cracks in those bricks I stacked up so high. And this crack? It just might be the biggest of all.

It's just occurred to me in this very moment that I want this baby. I *really* want this baby. I don't want to walk into that doctor's office and there not be a heartbeat.

"Great. Now *you* look scared too."

"I am," I say honestly, and her mouth drops open at my confession. "But I also know we don't have a thing to worry about. We're going to go in there and hear our baby's heartbeat, and everything is going to be just fine."

"How do you know?"

"Because I just do. And if I'm wrong, I'll let you hit me again. I know how much you love doing that."

"Ugh," she groans. "I can't believe I'm having a baby with you."

"Well, it's happening, so believe it, darlin'." I wink at her, and she rolls her eyes, but I see the smile playing on her lips. "Now come on, let's get inside before we're really late."

I push my door open but stop when I hear my name on her lips.

"Hey, Cameron?"

"Hmm?" I look back over at her.

She's peering up at me with unsure eyes.

She doesn't say anything for a long moment, just stares at me.

Then finally… "I'm glad it's you."

I hate that my throat grows tight and my eyes burn with unshed tears. Her words are like a punch to the gut and the absolute last thing I was expecting her to say.

I clear my throat and run my tongue across my lips.

"I'm glad it's you too, Hollis."

Pride swells in my chest as I stare out at the group of guys on the ice.

They look good. They look ready.

We're currently up three to one in our preseason game against Florida, and I knew the moment my skates touched the ice that this is exactly what I've been needing. To be out on the ice where I belong, to get my head back on straight and get immersed in the game I live for.

"Strong legs out there already," Collin comments, eyes trained on the same thing I'm looking at.

"Attaboy, Miller!" I yell as he flies by. Coach is testing him on some new lines this season, but he's looking good, looking sharp. "Keep this energy up and I think it'll be a good season."

"Spoken like a true captain," Rhodes says. He looks left and right, making sure nobody is paying us any attention, then leans in a bit. "You, uh, tell Coach yet?"

I shake my head, looking over at the short guy with the round belly, trying to picture the man who used to be an enforcer but finding it hard to see. "Not yet."

"You need to before the season starts."

He's right. I know he is.

I'm just not really looking forward to walking into Coach's office and telling him, *"Hey, remember that time I proposed to my girl because she was pregnant and we planned a wedding, and then it turned out she wasn't pregnant and it was a whole big thing? Yeah, well, this time I knocked up a one-night stand, and she's really knocked up this time. Oh, and, by the way, she's due in April."*

He's going to shit a brick.

"I will."

"Harper said things are going well," Collin comments out of the side of his mouth, eyes still tracking what's happening on the ice in front of us.

"Ryan even said you're going to appointments with her and got to hear the heartbeat yesterday," Rhodes adds.

"I heard you cried."

"I did not," I lie, because I swear to fuck I'm taking to my grave that after I dropped Hollis off at her apartment, I cried on my drive home. I felt stupid for it, but I still can't wrap my head around the fact that this is happening.

With Celine, it was different when she came to me saying she was pregnant. We'd been dating for months at that point. Sure, our relationship was still in that early honeymoon phase and there was still a lot of learning and growing to do, but we were committed to each other.

With Hollis, it's a whole different arena we're playing in now, and that's what scares me the most about it.

"I heard you wept like a little baby," Rhodes adds.

I did. "Fuck off." I scowl at them. "Is that all you four do? Just sit around and gab about my private life?"

"It's been the hot topic at the dinner table lately," Collin says. "I mean, you did get my sister-in-law pregnant. She and Harper talk a lot, you know."

"About anything good?" I'm only half-joking.

I'm curious as hell how the unfiltered version of Hollis is handling all of this. One minute I'm fine, the next I'm mildly freaking out. If I'm this back and forth, I can't imagine how she's feeling with the whole mix of hormones on top of it.

He doesn't get the chance to answer, because Coach puts us out on the ice. Rhodes and Collin pair up as per usual, and I fly by them, heading over for a pass we've practiced a thousand times. The puck hits just where I need it to, then I send it over to Smith, who taps it back as he tries to fight off Florida's man.

They're so preoccupied with defending against Smith they don't even realize I have the puck until the last minute, and by then it's too late. I bury it past their goalie, and the small crowd here at home goes nuts.

Sticks go in the air, and Smith smacks his glove against mine in celebration.

"Nice pass, man."

"Nah. That was all you." He's always so modest about his skills, but we all know he wouldn't still be playing in the NHL at his age if he didn't have the grit he does.

We clamber back onto the bench, catching our breaths, ready for our next run.

"Hey." Collin leans into me, his eyes locked on his defensemen. "What you said before? About if what she says about you is good or bad?"

"Yeah?"

"It's good, man."

I needed to hear that more than I thought I did.

"Good. That's…good."

"But I swear, if you hurt her, you're dead."

He doesn't have to be looking at me for me to know he's serious.

"I don't plan on it."

And that's the truth.

You can't hurt what you don't touch.

CHAPTER 11

HOLLIS & LOWELL

Lowell: I told Coach today.

Hollis: Did he freak?

Lowell: Only about the due date.

Hollis: What's wrong with the due date?

Lowell: We really need to talk about your lack of hockey knowledge.

Lowell: April is playoffs.

. . .

Hollis: Oh. And those are important?

Lowell: …

Hollis: I'm kidding!

Hollis: I know it's important because it determines the Super Bowl winner.

Lowell: I…I can't. I just can't.

Hollis: What? Something wrong? *bats lashes*

Lowell: I know you're just teasing, but words hurt, Hollis. They really, really hurt.

Lowell: I'm going to make it my sole mission to make you love hockey before this baby gets here.

Hollis: We'll see about that.

Lowell: How are you feeling?

Hollis: Fine.

Lowell: Just fine?

Hollis: I have a human growing inside of me that's depleting all my energy and making me a hormonal psycho.

Hollis: HOW DO YOU THINK I'M DOING?!

Lowell: Fine.

Hollis: You really don't need to keep checking in on me every day.

Lowell: It's MY human growing inside of you that's depleting all your energy and making you a hormonal psycho.

. . .

Lowell: Do you really think I'm not going to be checking in on you?

Hollis: Ugh. Fine. I get it.

Lowell: Thank you. And you're welcome.

Hollis: Welcome for what? This alien inside of me?

Lowell: Yes. But also for checking in on you.

Hollis: Please. Do NOT act like you're doing ME a favor. This is all your fault.

Lowell: It takes two.

Hollis: Lowell…

. . .

Hollis: Please. I'm tired. I can't take any more sparring today.

Lowell: Can you just let me know if you actually keep some food down?

Hollis: The doctor said it was fine and I shouldn't be worried.

Lowell: Okay. Then I'll worry for the both of us.

Lowell: Just text me, you stubborn woman, okay?

Hollis: Fine.

Lowell: Stop saying fine.

Hollis: Okay…

Hollis: Fine.

Lowell: Calliope

Hollis: No.

Lowell: Good.

Lowell: I hate that name.

Hollis: Then why did you suggest it?

Lowell: Just making sure we're on the same page.

Hollis: Speaking of page…

Hollis: What about Paige?

Lowell: I'm…indifferent.

.   .   .

135

Hollis: *eye-roll emoji*

Hollis: Of course you are.

Lowell: I have suggested no less than five names to you this week and this is the first time I've rejected one of yours and I get an OF COURSE?!

Lowell: Also, please note it wasn't an outright no. I just said I'm indifferent.

Hollis: That basically means no.

Lowell: *blinks*

Hollis: *blinks faster*

Lowell: *blinks hard AND faster*

Hollis: It's really rude of you to argue with a pregnant woman, you know. It causes stress for the baby.

. . .

Lowell: Leave her out of this.

Hollis: Or him.

Hollis: We still don't know yet.

Lowell: It's a girl. I can feel it.

Hollis: Oh, can you? Can you feel it? Even when it's not inside your body stealing all of your comfort and joy?

Lowell: Someone is a bit dramatic, no?

Lowell: Would it bring you joy if I had some food delivered?

Hollis: It would bring me joy if you left me alone.

Hollis: And sent a cheeseburger.

Lowell: You still pissed?

Hollis: Yes.

Lowell: Why?

Hollis: A SALAD, LOWELL. You sent me a salad. That's just…wrong. On many levels.

Lowell: One, I sent a salad because YOU were the one complaining about weight gain on the phone the other night.

Lowell: Two, I was reading a baby book and they said greasy foods probably aren't the best to consume. They're hard to digest. I did you a favor.

Hollis: Well, do me another favor—don't do me any more favors!

. . .

Lowell: That's a very counterproductive request, don't you think?

Hollis: Remember when I told you I didn't like you?

Lowell: Yes.

Hollis: Well, somehow, I like you even less today.

Lowell: I'll remember that for when I happen across a drive-thru and don't order you any ice cream.

Hollis: You wouldn't dare.

Lowell: Sorry. I can't text. I'm busy ordering food.

Hollis: Shut up and get me chocolate.

Hollis: NO! Swirl.

. . .

Hollis: Wait. Chocolate.

Hollis: Lowell?

Lowell: This is an automated message. The person you are trying to reach is currently in the drive-thru waiting on one small ice cream for nobody else but himself. Please try again later.

Hollis: I hate you.

Lowell: You wish.

Hollis: Sucks you guys lost tonight.

Lowell: You watched the game?

Hollis: No. Harper did.

Hollis: I just happened to be there.

. . .

Lowell: You totally watched.

Hollis: Did not. I don't even like hockey, remember?

Lowell: Take that back.

Hollis: It's boring.

Lowell: Hollis…

Hollis: And slow.

Lowell: Slow?! Are you kidding me? I can literally skate faster than the speed limit in my neighborhood!

Lowell: I can't believe I'm having a baby with a hockey hater. I'm so ashamed of myself.

Hollis: You are not.

141

. . .

Lowell: You're right. But I should be.

Lowell: Did you know that our baby is the size of a pair of baby booties?

Lowell: Whatever those are.

Hollis: Are you looking at baby websites again?

Lowell: Yes. Since I'm not there, I like to know what you're experiencing.

Hollis: That's…actually kind of sweet.

Lowell: I know.

Lowell: It's also still smaller than the average dick, but I'll have to let Miller know that the baby is catching up to him fast.

. . .

Hollis: Umm…excuse me?

Hollis: Like a penis?

Lowell: Yeah.

Hollis: Did you just compare our child to a penis? A PENIS?

Lowell: Again, yeah.

Hollis: How… What… Why do you know the size of the average dick?

Lowell: All guys know it instinctually.

Lowell: It's a thing. Trust me.

Lowell: Speaking of…how do we feel about Dick?

. . .

Hollis: I take it back. You're not sweet.

Lowell: I'm guessing Richard is out of the question, then, too?

Lowell: Hollis?

Lowell: Fine. I'll stop. But it's going to be really HARD to do.

Hollis: If you think I'm above kneeing you in the balls, I'm not.

Lowell: Oh, I am very well aware of all the pain you enjoy inflicting on me.

Hollis: Good. Now remember that the next time you compare our child to a penis.

CHAPTER 12

HOLLIS

"So, are you excited about your first professional hockey game?"

Not that I'd admit it to him anytime soon, but Lowell's project to make me love hockey by the time the baby gets here is actually moving along a lot faster than I thought it would.

Though I do think I owe more of the credit to Harper than I do to him. She's been making me watch all the preseason games and explaining everything to me. I still don't really understand it, but I will admit it's fun to watch.

"I…think so?"

I look around the big, nearly empty arena with wide eyes. Most people are still milling about the concourse buying merch and filling up on beer and food before warm-ups begin. This place is huge, and I can't believe it's about to be packed with 20,000 screaming hockey fans.

I'm proud of myself for keeping my hormones in

check because I've only had to excuse myself to the bathroom one time for crying when I came across a little girl with dark hair and pigtails who had LOWELL and the number 55 stitched across her back. She was so cute, and all I could think was... *That could be mine.*

"Just wait until the game starts. You're going to totally fall in love with it then," my sister says. "I didn't think I'd ever be into it, and now I love it."

I want to point out that she most likely loves it so much because her husband plays, but I don't.

"And it's going to make you so horny," Ryan adds. "Like, unbelievably so. Your sex drive is probably already off the charts, so I bet by the time we get done with this game, you are going to want to climb your man like a pole."

I'm a little surprised by how right she is about my sex drive being totally off the charts. I have woken up no less than four times this week from very vivid sex dreams—so vivid I've had to get myself off each time or else there was no way I was going to be able to go back to sleep. I know they say some women's sexual desires can be really intense during pregnancy, but I did not expect it to be *that* intense.

Just like I did not expect the star of my dreams to be Lowell, but *oh* has he been the star.

The most frustrating part of it all is that no matter how hot my dreams are, they still pale in comparison to the real thing, and that's something I have to live with every day.

"He's not my man."

Ryan and Harper look at each other and do very little to conceal their smirks.

"He's not my man," I insist, annoyed by their smiles. "There is nothing remotely relationship-y or intimate happening between us. We're just friends."

"Much to your vagina's dismay, I'm sure. I bet it would love to be dicked down by him."

"Ryan!" Harper hisses, looking around to make sure nobody heard her.

"Sorry. Ignore me. Hockey makes *me* horny, and I'm not even the pregnant one. It's just so"—she shimmies her shoulders—"*hot*."

"She always gets like this during the game," Harper explains. "I swear, she and Rhodes go at it like rabbits when it's over."

"I can definitely confirm that, but don't you dare sit there judging me like that when you know you and Collin do the same."

Harper's cheeks stain red, not denying it at all.

"Can we please stop talking about sex? Ryan was right—my libido is a little nuts right now and I can't do anything about it, so hush."

"Why can't you do anything?"

I point to my stomach. "Um, hello."

"Yeah, so?"

"Who is going to want to sleep with a pregnant woman?"

"Um, probably your baby daddy."

I wrinkle my nose. "I'm not sleeping with Lowell."

"Why? Scared he'll get you pregnant?"

I roll my eyes. "No. I'm not sleeping with him *because* he got me pregnant."

"Okay…" She draws the word out, clearly confused.

I sigh. "I can't sleep with him because we're not together, Harper. Yes, he got me pregnant, but we're not dating or anything."

"Remind me again why you're not."

"Because he doesn't do serious."

"I'd say having a baby together is pretty serious, Hollis."

"You're right. It is—but it's not like this was planned. We weren't even supposed to see each other again."

"But now you are seeing each other again and you're pregnant with his baby."

"Yeah…"

"So, then, what's the big deal if you sleep together? You're not going to hook up with other people while you're pregnant, are you?"

"No! Of course not!"

"Okay. Then…"

"Then what?"

"Then ride that dick while you can!" Ryan says.

Harper hitches her thumb toward Ryan. "Yeah, what she said."

"I… Okay. I'll take that into consideration."

I won't take it into consideration though. Lowell and I haven't really talked about our relationship or exactly how it is we're going to raise this baby, but I don't think we need to. He was clear from the start—he doesn't want a relationship. He already made the mistake of throwing himself into something he wasn't entirely ready for once, and he got hurt. He's not going to make that same mistake again.

The roar of the crowd pulls our attention, and Comets start spilling out for warm-ups, starting with their goalie. They step onto the ice one by one and skate in circles on the half of the rink closest to us.

Collin and Rhodes almost immediately come over to right in front of where we're sitting, and it is absolutely adorable to watch Harper and Ryan fangirl over their husbands while wearing their numbers on their back.

A sudden rush of jealousy rises in me. I don't understand what it means or where it's coming from, so I push it down and pretend it never happened, then focus my attention back to the ice.

I take it all in, absolutely mesmerized by everything that's happening. I have no idea how they are all successfully ignoring the people beating on the glass and trying to get their attention with signs and screams and everything else while also warming up for the game. How they're blocking it out, I have no clue, but it's impressive.

Even though I've only seen pictures of him in uniform and probably couldn't pick him out if I tried, I know the moment Lowell steps onto the ice because the Comets fans go nuts for their captain.

But he doesn't pay any attention to them.

No.

He looks at me.

In fact, he skates right over to me and stands at the glass, that stupid grin of his that is really starting to grow on me firmly in place. He tips his head and mouths one word: *Good?*

I nod, loving that even when he's supposed to be focusing on his game, he's worried about me and the baby.

His grin widens, satisfied with that answer. His eyes drift down the front of me, lingering on my chest and then my belly—both of which are starting to grow— before he drags his gaze back up to my face. His stare has me wiggling against my seat.

He taps the glass twice with the end of his stick, then skates away.

I can feel eyes on me, and I turn to find Harper staring holes into the side of my head.

"What?" I ask.

She smiles, shaking her head slowly before turning her attention back to the ice.

But not before I hear her murmur, "Just friends my ass."

Ryan was right.

Very, very right.

The final buzzer just sounded, and I am hornier than

ever. Watching grown men skate around after a puck and shove on each other shouldn't be hot, not in the least. But somehow…it is.

Like really, *really* hot.

"Well…" Ryan says, fanning herself. "That was nice."

I laugh, because *same*.

"We going to Slapshots?" Harper asks.

"What's Slapshots?"

"A sports bar that's just around the corner. They have a tradition of going after every home opener," Ryan says. "We can walk there. The guys will meet up with us in a bit after all the hubbub."

So that's what we do. We make our way a few blocks over and grab a table, and I learn that "hubbub" means their post-game interviews, a quick workout—which totally blows my mind—and reviewing what went wrong and what went right.

I'd say since they finished the game five to one and won the 15th consecutive home opener of their existence, there was a lot that went right.

We're not seated at Slapshots long before the guys file in. Everyone cheers when they're spotted, then returns to their respective drinks, and I like that they have a place they can hang out like this and not be bothered for the most part.

The bartender brings over several beers before the guys even have a chance to sit down, already knowing what they want.

"Hey, Rod. Can we get some sparkling water with lemon whenever you get the chance?"

He looks confused by Lowell's request, but when Lowell nods toward me, understanding dawns, and he nods, taking off to prepare the drink.

"Thanks," I say to Lowell as he takes the empty seat next to me, trying hard to ignore how good he looks and smells right now. He has a ballcap flipped backward and is wearing jeans and a shirt with #55 on the chest. Simple, but with the confidence and high he's riding after winning tonight, he looks ten times hotter.

Or maybe that's just the horniness talking again.

He winks in response, and I have to fan myself because my face instantly heats.

"You good?"

"Yeah, just…hot. And a little tired."

"We don't have to stay long, just a beer and then we can go. I was going to ask if you wanted to come back to my place tonight. Just to…you know…check it out, make sure it's all good for the baby and everything," he rushes out. "But if you're too tired—"

"I'm not," I say way too quickly. "I'm not too tired. That sounds…good. Nice."

"Good. Nice." He smirks. "Okay."

And that's exactly what we do.

Lowell has one beer before pushing away from the table, holding his hand my way. "You ready?"

I nod and slip my hand into his, allowing him to help

me from the chair. I try to ignore the fact that he doesn't let my hand go.

"We're heading out," he announces to the table.

"Aww, already?" Miller complains, poking his bottom lip out. "Boo."

"Sorry. I need to get my girls home. They're tired."

Harper perks up at his words. "Girl*s*?!"

"Ignore him. We don't know what we're having yet. He just thinks he knows it's a girl."

"Because it is," Lowell insists.

I ignore him. "We've decided to wait to find out at the twenty-week mark."

"My money is on a boy," Collin says.

"Nah. I say girl," Rhodes chimes in.

"Team girl here too," Miller agrees.

"You're officially outnumbered." Lowell places his hand on my belly. "You hear that? You had better be a girl or you're grounded."

I gape at him.

It's the first time he's touched my stomach, and the first time he's talked to the baby. It surprises me—not just because we're in public and everyone is definitely gawking at us now, but because he does it with such ease, like it's the most natural thing in the world to him.

I like that it's natural. I like that it's natural a little too much.

"What?" he asks, and I realize I'm still staring at him.

"Nothing." I tear my eyes from his as I blink back the tears threatening to spill over. "Let's get out of here."

Lowell's house is a lot more modest than I pictured it being. He's an NHL player who makes more in a year than I'll probably ever see in a lifetime, and I thought his house would be stories tall on sprawling land with a million windows and marble floors.

Instead, he lives in a gated community on about two acres, and not a single home is gawdy or lavish. It just looks like a normal community for normal everyday people.

"I like your new car," I tell him, running my hands over the interior of his brand-new Audi SUV.

"I promised you I'd get a new one for the baby."

I grin because he did promise that, and I love that he kept his promise.

"Don't worry, Fiona is tucked safely in my garage. Figured it was too cold for her tonight."

"Oh, phew. I was *so* worried about her."

"I know you were."

He shoots me a grin as he pulls into a short driveway and clicks a button so the garage opens.

Maybe I'm just really ignorant on what hockey players do with their money, but I definitely didn't expect his garage to house his truck and that's it.

No, wait—that looks like a bag of golf clubs tucked back in the corner.

We climb out of the SUV, and he leads me into the house via the kitchen. A few smart lights kick on when we enter, and the first thing I notice is the open concept, which leaves the living room visible from every angle in the spacious cooking area. Despite the navy blue cabinets and sleek black granite countertops, the kitchen is bright and open. I bet it's even more gorgeous in the daytime. The living area contains a couch, a TV mounted to the wall, and two bookshelves lined with odds and ends.

Everything is so…modest.

"Not what you were expecting?" he asks as I take it all in.

"Not at all," I admit. "I thought there would be more gold."

He laughs. "Nah. More of a silver guy myself."

I grin. "It's a really nice house, Lowell."

"Thank you. I'd like to take all the credit for it, but I had a designer do it all. I just wanted something simple and sleek that didn't cost an arm and a leg in case I ever play somewhere else."

The possibility of that never even crossed my mind, and my heart begins to race thinking about him moving away.

"Is that something that's going to happen?"

"I plan to Sidney Crosby my career and play for one team, but it doesn't mean it's not a possibility."

My hand instinctively goes to my belly as if to protect my baby from that heartbreak.

He doesn't miss it.

"Follow me. I have something to show you."

He leads me down a dark hallway, not stopping until he reaches the door at the very end.

I lift my brows at him, curious.

"I know we haven't really discussed the mechanics of this whole situation—something we should probably sit down and do—but I've been working on something. You know…just in case."

He pushes the door open and flips on the light.

My jaw drops, unable to believe what I'm seeing.

It's a nursery.

Not just any nursery either—it's a beautiful one with a custom design of a midnight mountain-scape stenciled on the wall. The furniture is a soft gray and there are touches of gold and yellow throughout. There's a half-built crib in the middle of it all, which tells me he's the one putting everything together himself.

"You did this?" I ask, my eyes darting everywhere, not wanting to miss a single detail.

"Yeah. I've, uh, been working on it since the night you told me."

I don't know what I was expecting him to say, but it wasn't that.

"You…have?" He nods. "But you didn't… You said… You…"

"Panicked. I panicked, but not once in that entire conversation did I say I didn't want the baby or want to be part of their life. I have *always* wanted that, and I *will* always want it." He steps into me, his hands finding my bump for the second time tonight. He bends at the knees to meet my eyes. "This is *forever*, Hollis, and I'm all in."

One.

Two.

Three.

That's how many seconds I last before I crush my mouth to his.

CHAPTER 13

When I asked Hollis to come back to my place tonight, it wasn't for this. I wanted to show her that I'm ready, that I'm preparing.

I didn't mean for this to happen.

She kisses me harder, almost like if she does, I'll respond. I don't respond because I can't help but think of the last time she kissed me when she shouldn't have.

I place my hands on her hips, and she takes it as a sign, pressing into me more. For just a moment, I give in, pressing her back against the nearest wall and devouring her. I slide my knee between her legs, and she moans, rubbing herself against it.

I know it's wrong and we shouldn't be doing this, but I can't resist. I want to kiss her. I want to kiss her so damn badly. I have since the moment I saw her sitting at the bar the night she told me she's pregnant. I wanted to sprint across that restaurant and pull her into my arms and make up for leaving her behind, and I've wanted to kiss her every day since then.

But I haven't because that's not what this is about right now. It's about the baby, not us.

I wrench my mouth away and she follows, trying to kiss me again, but I hold her back firmly.

Her eyes are glassy, her breaths coming in short spurts as she blinks up at me. "What's wrong?"

"That's… This isn't why I brought you here."

"That's sweet, really, but I'm a big girl. I want this."

"But what if I don't?"

Her face drops. "Is it… Is it because I'm pregnant?"

"What?! No, no. That's not it *at all*. Hollis, you're…" *Incredible. Gorgeous. Courageous.* "It's not because you're pregnant."

She peers up at me, her eyes shiny still, but this time with unshed tears. Her chin wobbles a little as she asks, "Then what is it?"

"It's just…" I press my forehead against hers, squeezing my eyes shut. "This is already complicated."

"What is?"

"This…*us*…"

"I know." She sighs. "I know. It's just I…*ache.*"

It's like her words are tethered to my cock because the moment they leave her lips, I'm harder than I've ever been before. I couldn't stop myself if I tried.

"Please, Cameron." She moves her hips, her eyes fluttering shut as she rocks herself against my jean-clad thigh. "Please. It doesn't have to mean anything. I just need something. Anything."

I can be something.

I can be anything.

"*I need you.*"

Three words—three words and all the excuses I had fly right out the window.

Without another word, I slam my mouth to hers, then scoop her into my arms and march us through the house. I don't stop kissing her and I don't stop walking until I reach my bedroom. Not even when I lay her on the bed and fit myself between her legs do I stop. I don't stop until she's fucking herself on my thigh and crying for release.

"More," she begs. "I need more. *Please.*"

I kiss my way down her throat and sit back, lifting her along with me. As much as I love seeing her wear my number, I need to see her even more. I peel her t-shirt from her body and toss the material aside, gently pushing her back down. Her brown hair fans around her, her tits, which are filling out more and more, spilling from the cups of her bra.

All I can do is stare because she's fucking gorgeous. She's gorgeous just like this, and all I can think about is how much further she has to go and how I can't wait to watch her grow my child.

I love the idea so much that I kiss her, thanking her with my lips in a way I don't know how to do with my words. It's not long before she's rubbing herself against my thigh again, and I know if I don't get her relief soon, she's going to burst.

I kiss my way down her throat and past her breasts,

which I promise to spend more time on later. I press kisses over her belly, promising to worship that later too, and I don't stop until I hit the waistband of her jeans.

Then, I laugh.

"What's so funny?" she asks, sitting up to look at what I'm seeing.

There's a small hairband holding the button of her jeans done because her belly is too big to fit. It's ridiculous and adorable.

"Oh," she murmurs sheepishly. "That."

"Yeah, that." My shoulders shake harder.

She glowers and shoves at my shoulder. "Shut up! It's not funny. All of my good jeans were in the wash, and I couldn't get these to button." She groans, then shoves me again. "Just forget it."

She tries to wiggle off the bed, but I don't budge that easily.

"Move," she demands.

"No," I say, grabbing her wrists when she starts beating on my chest. I push until her back hits the bed, then bring her arms up over her head and hold them there.

"Let me go, Lowell."

"Oh, so I'm back to being Lowell now?"

"Yes, because you're a jerk."

"I am not."

"Are too."

"Am not. Now stop moving."

"You are so annoying. You're—"

I kiss the insult from her lips, and it takes all of two seconds before she's moaning and rubbing against me again. My cock is throbbing behind the zipper of my jeans, and I think I need a release just as bad as she does.

But not yet.

She groans when I pull my mouth from hers and trace the same path from before down her neck and over her breasts and belly. This time, the only reason I stop is to undo the makeshift button on her jeans.

She shoves onto her elbows to look at me. "What are you doing?" she mutters, her voice scratchy with lust.

"Tasting you." I peer up at her. "I can taste you, right?"

She gulps, trapping her bottom lip between her teeth with a nod.

I slide her jeans from her legs, trying not to laugh at her urgency to help me, then reposition myself between them, swiping my tongue over her before she has the chance to protest again.

"Unghhh," she cries out, arching off the bed. "Oh god. *More.*"

And I oblige.

I spread her pussy with my tongue, licking and sucking and getting my fill until she's practically fucking my face. Her hands crash into my hair, holding me to her as she has her way with me, and I've never been so happy to be used in my entire life. Her legs begin to shake, and I know she's close.

I keep the same pressure applied with my tongue as I

slowly slide two fingers inside of her. I hook them up, and that's all it takes.

"Cameron…" she moans, her legs shaking around my head as she comes apart.

I wait for her legs to stop trembling before I slip my fingers out of her and kiss my way back up her body. She's coated in a light sheen of sweat, and her hair is a mess. It reminds me of the first night we had together, and for a moment, I wish I had never walked away.

I roll until I'm on my back, dragging her along with me. She rests her head on my chest and lets out a contented sigh.

"Give me five minutes," she promises, her words sleepy and slurred.

Those five minutes never come and neither do I, but I've never been more satisfied.

"You can't be serious."

"I am."

Hollis puts her hands on her hips, and I try not to stare too long at the baby bump that's becoming more and more obvious every day.

It's not that I don't want to stare—I *really* want to—but if I stare too long, I'm afraid I'll do something like rush across her apartment and toss her up on the counter and have my way with her. Seeing my child grow inside her is doing something to me that I never expected.

I like it. *A lot.*

It's why I'm over here all the damn time now and can't remember the last time I spent more than one night in my own bed.

"You really don't want to find out?"

"No." She shakes her head, the loose bun on top of it bobbing around as she moves through the kitchen. "I want to be surprised. You're more than welcome to find out, but I don't want to know."

"I'm surprised."

"Why?"

I shrug. "I don't know. I just figured you had all these grandiose plans of prepping a baby room with a theme and colors and everything else."

"I did." I tip my head, not understanding what she's getting at. "Before, I mean," she elaborates. "With Thad."

Right. Her ex. Her ex who is a huge piece of shit and who I want to punch.

"Why not now, then?"

"I...I don't know. Maybe I'm picking up hockey superstitions or something, but since none of this is what I had planned for my life, I figured I might as well keep that going and just be surprised."

Everything over the last few months has been so insane that I almost forgot Hollis hasn't even been divorced for six months. I can't imagine how she must be feeling going from happily married to divorced to pregnant by a guy she barely knows all in the span of a year.

It has to be taking a mental toll on her.

"You want to know what I think?" I ask as she sets her fresh glass of water down on the table, climbs back into her spot on the couch, and pulls her computer back into her lap.

It's a game day for me, and sometime over the last few weeks, this has become our routine until I have to be at the rink. I come over and we lie around on the couch. Sometimes she'll work, sometimes I'll read, sometimes we'll talk, but mostly it's just about spending time together.

"What's that?"

"You just don't want to see if I'm right and it's a girl."

"Well, do you want to know what I think?"

"What's that?" I echo.

"I think I need to pee."

I mock gasp. "I am shocked. *Shocked!*"

"Always right when I sit down too." She rolls her eyes, setting her laptop aside, then rises from the couch. She teeters a bit, and I'm on my feet in an instant to catch her.

I grip her waist, holding her steady. "You okay?"

"Yeah," she says, "just a bit wobbly." She points to her belly. "Still getting used to this big thing."

"It's not big."

"Don't try to placate me, Lowell. I'm big."

"You're not. You look just the size of a bell pepper, or

a bottle of baby shampoo. Take your pick." Her brows scrunch together at my words. "Baby sites—they're weird."

"Ah." She nods, pushing away. "Be right back."

She slowly makes her way to the bathroom, and I don't dare sit down until she's shut the door behind her.

I don't like that she's unstable, but I guess I can also understand. Her body is changing so much every single day even if she can't always see it. It's…well, kind of fucking amazing if you ask me.

I flop back down on the couch and nearly knock her laptop off the cushion with the force. I manage to grab it before it crashes to the floor and, in the process, wake it up.

I know I shouldn't look. It's a total invasion of privacy.

But I do it anyway because pulled up on the screen is an apartment, and I think that might involve me just a little bit.

Is she thinking of moving? She hasn't mentioned it and I just forgot, has she?

I click around the page and check out the photos. It's…fine. Not exactly what I would want to live in, but then again, I have the luxury of being picky.

It's a two-bedroom and the rent is almost double what she's paying here, not to mention it's on the complete opposite side of town…and the arena, which means I'll be farther away from her and the baby.

I don't want to be farther away from her or the baby.

I…

Oh shit.

Does she want me to ask her to move in with me?

I like being with her. I like touching her. And I definitely like what we did last week at my house.

But that's all different than actually being in a relationship.

I'm not sure I'm ready for that even if we are having a baby together. It's one thing to love and care for the baby growing inside her. The baby can't hurt me. All the baby will know is how to love me.

But Hollis…she can do so much more damage than that. I'm not sure I'm ready to give anyone that power yet.

I hear the toilet flush, then the water turn on, so I click back to the first photo and drop the laptop back where she had it. I do my very best not to look guilty when she comes out of the bathroom, pretending to scroll through something on my phone.

"Ah, so much better. For like twenty minutes, I mean." She laughs at her own joke as she climbs back onto the couch.

I halfheartedly smile at her. She turns her attention back to her laptop.

Click.

Scroll.

Click.

Scroll.

I don't stop watching her.

I can't stop watching her.

She notices.

"Do you remember at Harper and Collin's wedding when I ordered that chocolate milk and you didn't make fun of me for it?"

"Yes."

"And remember how Emilia came over and she and I danced?"

"Yes. That's when I discovered you're a liar who loves Queen."

"Everybody loves Queen, Lowell. I'm pretty sure that's an actual law somewhere."

"I don't think that's how that works, but okay. Why are you asking about the wedding?"

"I was just wondering if you remember when you sat at the bar staring at me, watching me dance for like twenty minutes like a complete creep."

"You knew I was watching you?"

"You're kind of hard to ignore." She lifts a brow. "Anyway, I just wanted you to know you're doing it again."

"Doing what again?"

"Staring at me like a creep."

Fuck.

"It's your beauty. I can't get enough of it."

It's true, but it's not the only reason I'm staring. I'm staring because I'm scared she wants more and I might not be able to give it to her.

She snorts. "I hope hockey covers your vision insurance. You clearly need your eyes checked."

I frown. That's the second time just today that she's commented on her body, and I wonder if it's because she's embarrassed about the changes.

I sigh, then reach over and push her computer closed, stealing it right out of her hands.

"Hey! I was reading something!"

I set the laptop on the table. "What were you reading?"

"A…uh…an article! Ha!"

"Oh yeah?" I lift a challenging brow. "About what?"

"How to get away with murdering your baby daddy."

I can't help but grin.

Baby daddy.

Daddy.

I'm going to be a dad.

It's the first time I've heard the word in reference to me, and I like it—and not in a kinky way. I'm going to be some little boy or little girl's daddy, and I don't think it's fully sunk in yet. I'm not sure it *will* sink in until the baby is here.

It's…scary.

And exciting too.

But mostly scary.

I shake my head, pushing away all the thoughts trying to intrude, then focus back on the task at hand: crawling across the couch until I'm lying on top of her and we're fitted perfectly against one another.

"You can't murder me."

"You're right. Collin already called dibs."

"I can take Collin."

"Uh, the busted lip you had a while back says otherwise."

"No. The busted lip I had says I deserved what I got, not that I couldn't take him."

"Hmm. I'm betting on Collin."

"Oh?" I ask, dropping my head and running my nose along her jawline, taking in the scent that's completely her. "Is that so?"

"Mmm"—she moans when I run my tongue over the column of her neck, unable to stop myself from tasting her—"hmm. That's s-so."

I chuckle against her, loving how responsive she is. I press my hips into her, letting her *feel* everything she's doing to me, letting her *feel* that even if she thinks she's not attractive, I do.

I keep pressing kisses along her neck and her collarbone and her cheek and everything I can except for her mouth, all while I rock my hips into her. She whimpers every time my cock brushes just right between her legs, and she arches her hips up, seeking more contact.

"Hey, Hollis?"

"Hmm?"

I rub against her again. Another moan. I drag my lips away from her body and pull back, breaking our contact.

This time when she whimpers, it's pained.

"No. What are you doing? I—"

"Hush," I interrupt, staring down at her. "I need you to listen to me, okay?"

"Okay," she says, and I laugh because that is *not* hushing.

She tucks her lips together, a promise not to say anything else.

"You're beautiful." She opens her mouth, but I cut her off with a sharp glare and she clamps her mouth shut. "*Everything* about you is beautiful, even the parts you don't like. Hell, *especially* the parts you don't like. Those are my favorite because they need the extra love."

A smile starts to slip across her lips.

"What you're doing...growing this baby inside of you...it's magical. Sexy. *You're* sexy. I need you to realize that, okay? I need you to realize that seeing your stomach grow and knowing that's *my* baby in there is the hottest thing I have ever had the pleasure of witnessing."

She doesn't say anything, but she doesn't have to. I can see the tears sliding out of her eyes and into her hair.

"So the next time you decide to talk crap about yourself, I want you to remember that every time you do, my boner dies, and that's just a waste of a good boner."

A laugh bubbles out of her, and I capture it with a kiss, wanting to keep it for myself. I might not be able to give her everything she needs, like a relationship or a welcome into my home, but I can give her this right now.

I kiss her until my alarm goes off, reminding me I need to be at the rink soon.

Then I kiss her some more. And once again just before I walk out the door.

"If we win tonight," I tell her, "that's becoming my pregame ritual. It has to—for science."

She laughs and shakes her head. "Damn hockey players and their superstitions."

That night, we beat Seattle four to zero.

I never understood it before when the dads on the team would complain about being away from their wives and kids, but I get it now, and I have never been more excited for a plane to land in my life. I'm so damn excited I almost become one of *those* people—the clapper when the pilot successfully lands.

I don't care.

I don't care because I miss Hollis and I need to see her.

I realize I'm probably growing way too comfortable spending time with her, but I can't stay away. Whenever we're not together, I want to be. Whenever we are together, I never want to leave. I just like being around her, and it's not even all entirely related to her carrying my child.

I just like *her*.

I get it now, what Smith was talking about when he said he was learning what matters and what doesn't, what was missing and what wasn't.

Hollis is what I've been missing.

I realize that now as I stumble into her apartment building just after two AM. Our plane landed not too long ago, and though I kept telling myself it was too late to bother her and just needed to go home, I drove here anyway. Even though I kept telling myself to turn around and not get on the elevator, I did it anyway, and even though I promised myself I wouldn't knock on her door, that's exactly what I'm doing right now.

I rap my knuckles against the wood, and it's only seconds until I hear a shuffling coming from inside the apartment.

Hollis pulls the door open. Though her hair is rumpled, she doesn't look like she was sleeping at all. In fact, it looks like she was waiting up.

For me.

She's wearing a thin t-shirt that's pulled tight over her stomach, which I swear is even bigger than it was the last time I saw her. Her tits—which have gone up at least half a cup size—are straining against the fabric so much that her nipples are nearly visible through it. She's wearing a pair of tiny shorts and a look in her eye that says she's hungry...and not for food.

My cock instantly springs to life, straining against the dress slacks I didn't bother changing out of.

"Hi," she says quietly, her lips tipping up in the corner.

I grin back. "Hey."

She doesn't move, and I don't either.

Then suddenly we're both moving at once.

I have no idea who reaches for who first, but one second I'm standing outside her apartment, and the next I'm inside with her against the wall, her legs wrapped around me, our mouths fused together like kissing each other is what they were made for.

Not kissing her for four days felt like hell.

Kissing her for four seconds feels like heaven.

And I have no idea how I'm going to stop.

CHAPTER 14

HOLLIS

I shouldn't be waiting up for Lowell for several reasons.

1. I don't know what time he'll be getting back to North Carolina.
2. I have no idea if he's coming over here because it's not something we've discussed.
3. We're not together.
4. I'm getting too attached and I know I am.

Despite knowing all of this, I'm waiting up anyway.

I miss him. I miss hanging out with him and laughing with him. I miss scrolling through baby websites with him, getting ourselves all worked up over what's to come. I just miss…him.

Something changed between us that night at his house. Not just physically, but emotionally too. It was the first time I really got to see how invested in this he truly is. You can say you're going to do something all you want, but actions speak louder than words, and Lowell's action of building our baby a room definitely spoke volumes.

A knock sounds at my door, and I jump off the couch before I can think too much about why I'm so excited by the idea of seeing Lowell, then swing the door open.

A lot of the guys tend to change out of their suits when they're on the plane back home, but Lowell didn't tonight. He's wearing a perfectly tailored dark gray suit that makes his green eyes look even more captivating and a smirk that says he's come over for a reason.

He rakes his eyes down my body, and I swear I can feel his stare penetrating me between my legs just like his tongue did a few weeks back. We haven't had a repeat of that night, but I want one—*badly*. Especially after the many make-out sessions we've had since then. He always seems to pull back at the last minute when it's starting to get good, but tonight, I want more.

Tonight, I want him.

"Hi," I whisper.

"Hey," he says, that grin of his growing.

I have no idea how long we stand there staring at one another, just like I have no idea who it is that makes the first move. All I know is one second Lowell is standing outside my door grinning at me, and the next he has me pressed against the wall with his mouth fused to mine.

"God, I missed your mouth," he says against me.

I missed you.

But I don't say that.

Instead, I say, "I missed yours more."

Then he kisses me on said lips. He kisses me until I'm almost positive they'll be bruised tomorrow. Until I'm literally writhing against him, needing relief. Until I am so fucking turned on I'm going to explode if something else doesn't happen soon.

"Lowell…"

He chuckles darkly, like he knows what he's been doing to me all along. He goes to pull away, pumping the brakes like he has been doing, and I can't this time.

I *need* a release.

I clutch the lapels on his suit, not letting him run, and look straight into his deep green eyes, loving the way they darken as he begins to understand what I'm silently asking for.

Begging for.

He gulps once. Twice.

"Are you sure?" he asks quietly.

He's not asking me if I'm sure I want to have sex. We both know the answer to that. He's asking if I'm sure I understand what we're about to do really means.

Sex.

Just sex.

I know that, and he knows that too. He can't offer more, and I'm not even sure if I'm ready for more.

But this right now? This I am definitely ready for.

Just sex.

177

I want *just sex*.

"Yes."

His eyes flicker with just that simple word, then he's ravaging my mouth again.

We kiss for what feels like hours before he wrenches his mouth from mine, down my chin, and over my throat. He kisses me there, nipping and sucking, leaving behind spots that will surely be visible tomorrow, but right now I don't care. Not when his hand is sliding along my side, his fingers brushing the waistband of my shorts but never slipping beneath the tiny bit of fabric. Over and over, torturing me slowly. *Deliciously.*

I love and hate it, and I want more yet I want him to stop.

When he finally dips his fingers into my shorts, I sigh with the relief of what's to come.

Lowell slowly moves his fingers lower and lower until just the pad of his finger brushes over my clit. I hiss at the contact, and he laughs again like an asshole, clearly enjoying my discomfort.

He doesn't move his hand for a long time. He just holds the pad of his finger there, alternating between kissing paths up my neck and sucking on my lips.

Then finally—fucking finally—he dips a single finger into me, and my knees nearly buckle.

"Fuck, you're wet."

"Because you're torturing me!"

He chuckles again. "You like it."

"I do," I pant, bearing down on his finger that's

gliding in and out of me, loving the way his palm is brushing against my clit. "So much. But you know what else I'd like?"

"Hmm?"

"To be fucked."

He pauses for only a moment, then says, "I think I can manage that."

I cry out when he withdraws his finger from me, and then yet again when he lifts the glistening digit to his mouth and licks it.

"Shit," he groans. "I almost forgot how good you taste."

"You…like doing that?"

"Like it? Are you kidding me?" He laughs mockingly, one side of his lips turning up in a smirk. "I'd spend an entire twenty-four hours with my face buried in your pussy if I could."

I tremble at the thought, loving the idea of it, especially given the last time he was between my legs, I thought I was going to stop breathing at one point.

He doesn't miss the shiver.

"Is that what you want?" He cups me through my shorts. "For me to eat your pretty pussy?"

"Y-Yes. No. Yes."

He laughs. "Well, which one is it, darlin'?"

"What I mean is *yes*, but not now. Right now, I want…" I gasp as his thumb presses into me through my shorts, circling my clit with a force that's just delightful enough. "I want…"

"To be fucked, was it?"

I gulp, nodding.

He steps away—like *completely* away.

I reach for him, but he shakes his head just once. He kicks his shoes off, then, slowly, he shoves his suit jacket off his shoulders and tosses it aside. His hands drop to his belt, and I practically salivate watching him unhook it. He doesn't take his pants off though. He doesn't pull his cock out, and somehow, it's hotter than if he were actually naked.

His deft fingers make quick work of undoing the buttons on his dress shirt. He strips that off and throws it somewhere too.

He's gorgeous. There's no other word to describe it.

He reaches out, one finger under my chin, and tips it up.

"Don't move," he instructs, and I nod.

Then he's gone. Across-the-room gone.

He sits on the couch, spreading his legs wide, and just watches me. His eyes rake up and down my body, then he does it all over again. Just. Watching.

It's unnerving and exhilarating all at once. I've never been touched like this before, and he's not even physically touching me. He's just looking, and somehow, it's so much more.

"Strip." His voice is low and commanding, and it makes me eager to follow his directions.

I grab the hem of the thin t-shirt I have on and slowly tug it over my head. I'm not wearing a bra, and it feels so strange standing before Lowell with just a pair of shorts on.

When I don't make a move to push them off, he lifts a brow, waiting.

I want to make him wait.

I want to make him squirm and yearn for me like I am for him. So I take my messy hair and wrap it into a ponytail, loving the way the strands brush lightly across my shoulder blades. Loving the way his eyes track every single movement. Loving the way the humor dances in his eyes when he realizes what I'm doing.

Finally, when I'm good and ready, I drag the shorts down my legs, stepping out of them and tossing them to the side.

His eyes widen, then darken, and he inhales a sharp breath at the sight of me. He slides his pants down his legs, his cock finally springing free, and *oh god* is it as beautiful as I remember.

He strokes it once, twice, reaching down to cup his balls and pull on them. My nipples pebble to stiff peaks just watching him, and I bet if I were to slip my hand between my legs right now, I'd be drenched.

Only then do I realize I never had any power in this moment at all. It was all him.

It was always him.

"Come."

Slowly, I saunter across the room, enjoying watching him play with himself.

I stop at his knees. "Now what?"

"Now, you use me."

Use me.

He said that before, and just like then, it does something to me. I know it's him relinquishing control because he wants me to feel comfortable. I love that he's putting my comfort first. I think it's hotter than anything else that's happened tonight.

He reaches a single finger out, sliding it through my pussy for a moment, only to bring it back to his mouth for a taste.

I lied. *That's* the hottest thing he's done tonight, and it has me falling into his lap—literally. I straddle him, twining my arms around his neck and rubbing myself against him. He looks down, watching where we're connected.

"Fuck," he mutters. "You're perfect."

"I haven't even done anything yet."

His hands find my ass, kneading my cheeks.

"And if you don't soon, I may revoke the whole *being a gentleman* thing I'm doing."

I roll my bottom lip between my teeth. "I'm sorry, Lowell, am I teasing you too much?"

I rub against him again.

"Is this taking things too slow for you?"

Another rub.

"Is this—"

I don't finish the sentence.

I don't finish the sentence because suddenly I'm lifted and Lowell's cock is pushing into me.

We both let out a low groan as he slides in, inch by delicious inch.

I've missed this. It's the first thing that runs through my mind, which is ridiculous because I've only had *this* one other time.

I lean forward, resting my forehead against his, trying to get used to his size again.

"You feel…" He gulps. "*Fuck.*"

"Good fuck?"

"*Great* fuck."

He crashes his mouth to mine, kissing me slowly as he lets me take the lead, allowing me to slowly work myself on him. He doesn't rush me; he lets me have complete control.

My orgasm is building higher and higher and it's within reach, I just need…

"Lowell…"

His fingers that have been playing lightly in the ends of my ponytail are the only indication of what's to come. Suddenly, he wraps my hair around his fist and yanks my head back just hard enough for it to cause a bite of pain, but not enough for it to be malicious.

I cry out as his other hand comes up to rest at the base of my throat, where he applies just the tiniest hint of pressure as he fucks up into me. Over and over again. Faster. Harder. So damn needy I think I may actually fall apart.

And then I do.

My orgasm hits me out of nowhere, a blinding white

light behind my eyes and a tingle from head to toe. There was no warning. No usual crescendo. It just shattered the earth around me with no preamble.

My pussy clenches around Lowell's cock and he's riding the same wave I am just moments later, spilling himself inside of me. Almost instantly I collapse onto him, and he catches me with ease, like he knew it would happen all along. He wraps his arms around me as I rest my head on his shoulder, trying to catch my breath.

I have no idea how long we sit like that—Lowell holding me and drawing small circles on my back, me resting against him.

But however long it is, I know it's not enough.

Which isn't a good thing because this *has* to be enough.

With as much energy as I can muster, I push away, finally looking at the man who just made my world implode. His curious green eyes are watching me, searching to make sure I'm okay with what just happened.

I'm okay with it.

I am *more* than okay with it. *Too* okay with it.

"Well, the good news is, I definitely didn't get you pregnant this time."

A laugh bursts out of me because it's what I didn't know I needed right now.

But Lowell knew.

Lowell always knows.

And that's what scares me the most.

CHAPTER 15

I tried to resist her.

Heaven help me, I tried.

But it was impossible with her looking up at me with those sapphire blue eyes full of desire and need. So, I caved, and if it meant waking up with her curled around me like she currently is, I'd do it all over again.

Hell, I'd do it all over again even if she weren't. Last night was incredible. The kind of incredible that rocks you to your core and scares you because you're certain absolutely nothing will ever be that good again.

It can't be. It's impossible.

She wiggles against me, and I can tell by the change in her breathing that she's beginning to wake up, which means I should probably stop staring at her like a total creep.

"Mmm." She snuggles deeper into me. "You're warm."

"It's a blessing and a curse."

"I'm always cold."

"I've noticed."

She presses a soft kiss to my side, and I can feel her grin against me. It's the same dopey grin I'm wearing.

"Good morning," she mutters.

"Good morning. Sleep well?"

"Mmm," she says again, this time stretching her body out. "So good."

"Are you sore?"

"A little." She blushes. "But I like it."

I like that she likes it.

She pushes up on her elbow and looks down at me. "Can I try something?"

"Of course."

She leans down and presses her lips to mine. It's a quick kiss before she's pulling away, but I grab her, holding her hostage before she can get too far.

"We've tried that before," I say to her.

She laughs. "We have, but you'll thank me later."

She kisses me again, but this time, she doesn't pull away—she heads south.

And keeps going and going.

She pauses when she reaches my stomach.

"Is that… Is that *lint* in your belly button?" She digs the piece of fuzz out, tossing it onto the floor.

"Hey! Put that back! It was keeping me warm."

"You're ridiculous." She smothers a laugh against my stomach, continuing her path.

She looks and feels fucking amazing, sliding over me,

pressing kisses down my stomach. Her pussy slides against my cock as she continues her languid assault, and I'm only mildly embarrassed by the sound that leaves my throat.

She laughs, then places kisses all over my thighs, dutifully ignoring my cock that's likely harder than it's ever been in my life. I would do anything in this moment to feel her pretty lips wrapped around it.

She kisses my right thigh, then my left. Back to my right, but this time she's just slightly closer to my balls. She keeps going until I'm pretty sure I'm going to nut without her ever touching my dick.

Then, in one slow, long lick, she traces her tongue from my balls all the way to the tip of my cock and finally covers it with her mouth.

As embarrassing as it is, I almost come.

"*Fuuuuuuuck.*" My hips rise involuntarily.

She giggles around me, and I swear to fuck I feel it in my toes too. She sucks me, rolling her tongue around the head, using one hand to fist my length and the other to lightly scrape her nails along the sensitive inside of my thigh.

I'm going to die.

I am going to die, and this is going to be the most epic death ever.

I don't even notice I've driven my hips upward until she gags, and I immediately feel bad, backing off.

"Shit. Fuck. I'm so sorry. I—"

She shoves me back down, continuing to work me

over, and it's not long until I build right back up to where I just was—about to make a mess.

"I'm going to come, Hollis, so unless you want me—"

"Use me," she murmurs, repeating my words back to me.

She wraps her tits around my hard cock and opens her mouth. She wants me to fuck her tits.

Oh god.

So, I do.

I fuck her tits, loving the way the tip of my cock brushes against her tongue. Everything is just enough to make me explode.

"Incom—"

It's all I can manage before I coat her lips and throat and her chin with my cum, and I'd be lying if I said the sight of her covered in me wasn't enough to make me ready for another round right away.

Because it is. I'm not exactly sure why it is, but it's hot and it's doing something to me.

She pushes up to her knees, looking up at me with a proud smirk.

"You good?"

I laugh, throwing myself back on the bed as she crawls back up to the pillows. "I can't believe I just fucked your tits. That's like shit you do when you're eighteen and your girlfriend is on her period, but you want to screw and she says no to anal, so you go to town between her tits."

"That sounds…oddly specific." Hollis lifts an amused brow.

I shrug. "Just some story I heard from some guy."

"Uh-huh." She laughs. "Sorry we didn't… I'm just tired."

My brows crush together. "Hollis, you don't need to apologize, and you also don't need to titty-fuck me because you feel too tired for sex."

"Well, I wanted to. So there."

"Is that your way of saying no to anal?"

She sputters out a laugh. "Yes. Yes, it is."

"Yet…right?"

She shakes her head with a grin, rolling away from me. "Don't you have practice this morning?"

Oh fuck.

I scramble to check the time, but it's still early. Like way-too-early-to-be-up kind of early.

But I have an idea.

"Come on," I tell her. "I want to take you somewhere."

"Is it to the shower? Because…" She looks down at the mess drying on her.

"Yes. And then to donuts."

"Donuts?" She dashes off the bed faster than I've seen her move in weeks and runs to the bathroom. "I'm showering first!" she calls out, and I laugh.

We are definitely not taking turns.

"*This* is the place you've been getting donuts from?"

"Yep. Why?"

"I don't know. I guess I just wasn't expecting an adorable food truck. I thought it would be a little mom-and-pop shop or something."

"Nah. Just Scout."

She lifts a brow. "Scout? You're on a first-name basis with the donut maker?"

"You jealous?"

"No," she says quickly…*too* quickly.

I try not to think too much about how much I like the idea of Hollis being jealous of another woman over me. Not that she has a reason to be, but still.

"Right. Sure." I wink. "Stay there."

I round the truck and pull her door open, helping her down.

"You don't have to do that, you know. I am perfectly capable of exiting a vehicle by myself. I'm pregnant, but not *that* pregnant."

"Are you seriously complaining about me being a gentleman right now?"

"I—well, no. Kind of." Her cheeks darken as we make our way up the path to the food truck turned donut shop.

"I was raised with manners, Hollis, and pregnant or not, I'll still help you out of the truck. Because that's what *gentlemen* do."

She presses up on her tiptoes to whisper, "Do *gentlemen* also do what you did to me this morning?"

Don't get a boner.

Don't get a boner.

Do. Not. Get. A. Boner.

"Behave," I mutter, both to her and myself because I know I *really* don't want to behave right now.

We get into the back of the line. It's short today. Usually, this place is about ten people deep every time I come here. I have no idea how Scout keeps up with everything, but she always does.

"So, how'd you find out about this place?" Hollis asks, taking in the little setup.

"Well…I grew up about two hours from here, and Scout went to high school with me. She's two years younger and was in the same grade as my sister. Word got out back home that she owned this place, so I made it my mission to come by and support it as much as I can. I might also make sure to cause a scene when I'm here and get my picture taken as much as possible in hopes it makes it on social media and gets her some of the recognition she deserves."

What I don't tell her is that Scout was bullied a lot for being shy and for having gay dads, and I couldn't stand the thought of her putting her all into this business and having it fail, not after everything she's gone through.

Hollis tips her head to the side, studying me. She doesn't stop, not even when I shift uncomfortably under her gaze.

"What?" I ask.

"Nothing. It's just… You're a good guy, Lowell."

"Are you surprised by this?"

She takes a moment to answer, and that's how I know it's honest and not a reflex. "No."

That makes my heart swell with pride.

"Mr. Lowell!"

A little voice pulls my attention from Hollis, and I look over to find the eight-year-old who believes we're the best friends in the world charging at me, a sketchbook and pencil in her hand as usual.

To be fair, she's right—we *are* the best friends in the world.

"What'd I tell you about calling me Mr. Lowell?" I ask as she skids to a stop in front of me.

"That it makes you sound like your dad and you ain't no old man."

"That's right." I hold my fist out, and she bumps it. "What are you doing here today, Miss Macie? No school today?"

"Nope. I have the day off because the teachers gotta talk to the mommas and pappas."

"Are they talking to *your* momma and pappa?"

She shakes her head adamantly. "No! I've been good!"

"No more kicking?"

She puts her hand on her hip. "Only when the boys need it."

I tuck my lips together, trying not to laugh. "That's fair."

"Who's this?" She points to Hollis. "This your

girlfriend?" The word girlfriend comes out with the slightest hint of disdain, and neither I nor Hollis miss it.

"I'm Lowell's...friend," Hollis tells her, sticking her hand out to shake it.

Macie looks at it, then back at Hollis. "*I'm* Lowell's *best friend.*"

"Oh, so *you're* the one he's been telling me all about, huh?"

I grin because I know she's just trying to make Macie feel important. I've never mentioned her to Hollis before at all.

Macie's little eyes widen. "He talks about me?"

Hollis nods. "All the time. He was telling me what a good artist you are too."

"I *am* a good artist. You want to see?"

"I would love to." Hollis turns back to me. "Grab us girls some donuts, will ya?"

She winks, then lets Macie drag her away to a table nearby. I watch as they go, stepping up to the front of the food truck to order.

Scout being Scout, she already has my usual ready to go.

"Can I get a chocolate milk and a Boston cream too?"

I catch her grin from the corner of my eye, then finally look over at her.

She's watching me with a look I can't quite decipher, and I don't know how I feel about that. I've known Scout from a distance for a long time now, and we've even been friendly over the last few years. I don't like that I can't quite read this expression when I usually always can.

"What?"

She shakes her head, raising her hands. "Nothing."

"Bullshit. That's a something look."

"What's that you're doing with her, Lowell?"

"With who?"

Scout nods toward the table where Macie and Hollis have their heads bent together, discussing whatever it is they're drawing. They look so cute, and with Macie's dark hair, they almost look like they could be mother and daughter.

That's going to be mine someday.

The thought hits me all at once, and I'm taken aback by it.

I know logically, this *will* be mine someday. But not *mine* mine.

And the thought that I want it to be terrifies me.

I slide my card toward Scout. "It's nothing."

Her brows rise, the corners of her mouth tipping up. "Then my look was nothing too."

We're both full of shit, and we both know it.

CHAPTER 16

HOLLIS

"I'd like to keep an eye on your morning sickness, but everything is looking good. Your fundal height is about twenty centimeters."

"Her fungal is what?"

"Fun*dal*," I correct Lowell, trying not to laugh because he looks incredibly concerned. "She means the distance from my pubic bone to my uterus."

"Twenty centimeters…that's like seven and a half inches or so, right?"

"A little over, yes."

He nods. "And that's good?"

"Yes. It's measuring in range. Now, would you like to find out if you're having a boy or a girl today?"

"No."

"Yes."

We answer the doctor at the same time, and she laughs at our difference of opinion.

"Seems we have a split."

If there's anything we've discussed the most during

this pregnancy, it's wanting to know or keeping it a surprise. I am team surprise while Lowell is dying to know, though I think that's mostly because he wants to prove me right if the baby is a girl.

I always thought I'd want to know too, but as the weeks go by, I realize it truly doesn't matter to me what we have. All I want is to be able to look into that baby's eyes and say, *"I love you."* The rest doesn't matter, and it will never matter.

"Is that normal?" Lowell asks from the chair beside me.

He's sitting forward, elbows resting on his knees, observing everything happening. It's the same stare I've seen from him when he's watching anything hockey related—serious and studious.

Even with the season in full swing, he's been so attentive and present. Hell, he showed up for this appointment today still wet from his shower after morning skate, and then when this is over, he'll go back to the rink for a game tonight.

It shouldn't surprise me, but it does. Something tells me if I were having this baby with anyone else, they wouldn't be this invested, and that makes me feel ways I know I shouldn't be feeling.

"It's pretty common," the doctor says reassuringly. "Plenty of parents are opposite on the decision to know or not. How about I put it in an envelope and whoever wants to know can look? Sound good?"

"That's perfect," I answer, then look at Lowell. "You happy?"

"Yes. I can't wait to see that I'm right."

The doctor laughs and continues with the exam. When we're finished, she tells us everything looks perfect and she'll see us for our next appointment, then sends us out front to set it up.

"My penis."

"What?!" I squeak out, eyes widening, glancing at the receptionist who either isn't paying us any attention or is really good at acting. I gulp, looking back at the man I just might murder today. "W-What about it?"

"Your fundal height is the size of my penis. Seven and a half inches."

I don't have to look in a mirror to know my cheeks are on fire right now. "Cameron!"

"What? It is."

"That's...nice." I peek back over at the receptionist, who, based on how red *her* cheeks are, is now listening *very* intently to our conversation. I lower my voice. "You couldn't have found literally anything else to compare that measurement to? Literally *anything* else that's seven inches?"

"*Seven and a half.*" He shrugs. "I'm sure I could have, but I'm most familiar with this one."

"That's... Okay, all right."

I shake my head, promising with my eyes to make good on that homicide threat. I turn back to the receptionist, who looks like she wants to both laugh and climb on top of Lowell to see if he's lying or not.

"Our appointment," I snap, and even I'm surprised by how bitchy I sound.

"Oh! Of course!" She scrambles around to get us scheduled for our next visit and gives us a card with all the information.

Lowell sets his hand on my lower back as we leave.

"I liked that," he says quietly.

"Hmm?"

"Your jealousy."

"I wasn't jealous," I lie. "I was just…ready to leave."

He lifts his brows and tucks his lips together, clearly not believing me as he steers me toward the truck— because yes, he is still driving the clunker around—and opens the door for me. He helps me climb inside, and by the time I sit down, I'm winded, because that's just my life now.

I sigh, leaning back against the seat.

"You doing okay?" he asks, going from laughter to concern as he searches my eyes for an answer.

"Yeah, just…tired."

He's always doing that, always staring and looking at me, like *really* looking at me. Sometimes it's unnerving, and sometimes I like it entirely too much.

I'm starting to realize I like a lot of things about him entirely too much.

I like how patient he is and how supportive he is. How

funny and smart and kind he is too. I like the way he looks at me from across the room, and I like the way he touches me like he's not able to not touch me. I like the way I feel when I'm with him—protected and cared for.

And I really like the way he loves our baby.

He crowds against me, sliding his hands up my thighs to my protruding belly.

I can't stand anyone else touching it. I've had some people try in the grocery store—creepy much?—and it's uncomfortable even during the exams. Hell, not even Harper has touched it.

But when it's Lowell's hands on me, it's calming, and I almost crave the calm.

"You sure that's it?"

"I'm sure."

He nods, then dips his head, putting his lips near my belly. "Excuse me, little miss, but you're wearing your mom out and that's my job, okay?"

He places a gentle kiss to my belly, and now I'm no longer tired—I'm turned on. There's something about seeing him talk to our baby that drives me wild, and he's been doing it more often lately, which means I've been ripping his clothes off more.

We've not really talked about us sleeping together, but we're not *not* talking about it either. It's just sort of…happening.

I want to ask him what it means—if anything—but I don't want to ruin whatever it is we have going on either.

I just want to enjoy it and get through these last few months of my pregnancy.

"Are you quite finished?" I tug him back up. "You know it gets me going when you go all *daddy* on me." I let out a squeak. "Not like *daddy* daddy. But *daddy*, the non-kinky kind of daddy."

His eyes dance with laughter. "Duly noted."

"Shut up," I grumble, totally embarrassed. "Are you going to open that envelope or not?"

He dips his hand into his back pocket and pulls out the envelope containing the anatomy scan of our baby.

He wiggles it my way. "Are you sure you don't want to know?"

"I'm positive. Don't tell me. Don't give any indication if you're right—which you're not—or if I'm right—which I am. But you can look."

He slips his finger into the envelope and peels it open, pulling out the scan just enough to see the results.

And then nothing happens.

There is not a single twitch on his face when he sees it. I watch more closely than I've ever watched anything before, but he gives nothing away. He simply slips the scan back in the envelope and places it back in his pocket.

All that curiosity I've been pushing away for months comes barreling into me, and I want to reach in there and rip open the scan and see it for myself right this moment.

He laughs. "You totally want to know now, don't you?"

I growl at him. "Again, shut up."

Another laugh.

I groan. "Don't you have a hockey game to play or something?"

"No, *darlin'*, I have a hockey game to win."

"Please tell me that glow you have going on is not just pregnancy but because somebody got dicked down by the hot-as-hell hockey player who knocked her up."

Sparkling water sprays out of my mouth at her words. "Jesus, Emilia." I run the back of my hand across my lips to clean them up. "Ryan said that before. Who says *dicked down*? What does that even mean?"

"You know when he lays you down, then bangs you so good you can't walk straight for at least two days? That's getting *dicked down*."

I sputter out a laugh. "Oh my god, what is wrong with you?"

She shrugs, brushing her long red hair out of the way. "I'm horny and it's been forever since I have personally been dicked down myself. I'm sure working with all these hot players isn't helping at all. It's starting to get to me."

"I'm sorry." And I am sorry. I know what it's like to be around Lowell all day long and not get *dicked down*, so I understand.

"It's fine. It's my own fault." She waves me off. "Anyway, you didn't answer my question. Is that a sex glow and not a baby glow?" She takes a sip of her wine, eyeing me expectantly.

I go for a noncommittal shrug, but I've known Emilia since the first grade, and she knows exactly what all my shrugs mean.

"Ha!" She points at me. "You totally got laid, didn't you?"

I roll my lips together, nodding. "I did. I got laid a lot. Like *a lot* a lot."

"Wait—has this been going on a while?" She pulls a frown when I nod. "I feel so bad that I haven't been around, but it's—"

I wave my hand. "It's the middle of hockey season. I understand, and it's not a big deal. I know you're busy corralling grown-ass men who love to throw themselves around on the ice. You have a life and a job. I get it. Me, I'm just kind of here, waiting to have this baby and looking for a bigger apartment and hoping I can bust my ass over the next few months so I can afford said bigger apartment when the baby comes."

I found a place that's almost directly in between Lowell's and the arena. It's decently within my budget with a little tweaking, but I know I'm going to have to put in double the time I usually do over the next couple of months to be able to save up money for any kind of maternity leave.

I also know it's going to be a lot of extra hard work

for me when the baby comes because Lowell is about to be in the most important part of his season.

She tips her head. "What do you mean? Why aren't you just moving in with Lowell?"

"Why would I move in with him?"

"Uh, because he got you pregnant!"

"Yes, I am aware of that fact."

"And you're sleeping together!"

"Again, yes, aware of that."

"You're telling me you're sleeping together, you're pregnant with his baby, and you're not going to move in with him?"

"Yeah, pretty much."

She doesn't say anything for several long moments. She just watches me, and it's unnerving because when Emilia just watches, it means whatever she says next is something I know I am not going to like.

"You're insane," she whispers. "This baby has sucked all of your brain cells out of you and you have gone utterly insane."

To an extent, she's not wrong. But that's not what this is about. "I don't see what the big deal is."

"You don't see what the big deal is…" She mutters my words back to herself, then scoffs. "Come on. You're smarter than that, Hollis. I know you are."

I am. But I'm also dumb enough to keep doing it.

I wave her words off. "It's fine. I'm fine. *We're* fine."

"Are you?"

"Yes!"

It comes out louder than intended, but I'm getting frustrated by her line of questioning. I'm a grown adult. I know what I'm doing.

"Sorry," I say. "It's just… We are both very aware of what this is. It's the same score as last time. It's nothing serious."

She looks pointedly at his shoes that are sitting by the door.

"I admit that does look a little serious, but that's not what this is. We are just two people enjoying the company of one another while we wait on our baby to come into this world. I don't have any preconceived notions about what is happening between us, and I know Lowell also does not have any preconceived notions about what's happening between us. In case you forgot, I haven't even been divorced for a full year. I am not looking to rush into anything serious." I run my hand over my belly. "Well, besides my baby, of course. But it's not like I can just return that one. I didn't keep the receipt."

She laughs lightly, but the joy slips from her penetrating gaze all too soon. "Can I say something?"

"Knowing you, you will anyway." I motion for her to continue.

"I spend a decent amount of time around the team. Yeah, I don't travel with them often, but I'm here at home with them when they're at the rink, which we both know is a lot of hours a day during the season. So, it's safe to say I know these guys fairly well, which means I

204

feel like I can say this with confidence: I have never seen Lowell the way he is now."

"What do you mean the way he is now?"

"I mean...lighter. Happy." She takes a sip of her wine. "Don't get me wrong—he's always been really nice and friendly and he's just an all-around really good guy. But he's also always been private and a little guarded, especially when it comes to letting anybody get close to anything about his personal life. That said, I can't tell you the number of times I have witnessed that man pass around a photo of your sonogram with nothing but pride on his face, just like I can't tell you the number of times I have seen his face light up talking about not just your baby, but you. I say that as a person who has seen this without even knowing you two were sleeping together, which means I'm coming from the standpoint of pure honesty when I say he has feelings for you."

I sigh. "Of course he probably has some feelings for me—I'm carrying his baby."

"True, but..." She lifts her shoulder. "I don't know, Hollis. It's different. *He's* different. Even if neither one of you are ready to admit it, he has *feelings* feelings for you, and unless you somehow end up admitting them, neither one of you are walking away from this unscathed in the end."

"End? There is no end, Emilia. I'm the mother of his child."

She lifts her wine to her lips and raises her brow. "I know, and that's the bitch of it all."

CHAPTER 17

I could stand here and watch this all day.

That's what flits through my mind as I lean against the wall just inside Hollis' apartment, watching her shake her ass from across the room. I remember the first time I watched her dance, and I remember thinking she was godawful at it then.

She still is. And yet, I still love watching her.

"Radio Ga Ga" by Queen is blasting out of a smart device on the counter, and she has no idea I'm even standing here. She's using a wooden spoon as a microphone and singing horribly off-key.

It's adorable. *She's* adorable.

I don't alert her to my presence until the song fades out.

"Very nice! Encore!" I clap my hands.

Apparently, it's the wrong thing to do.

"SON OF A...!" She whirls around, hand to her chest. "Lowell! I just pissed myself, you ass!"

She takes off running for the bathroom and slams the door, all while muttering to herself.

I won't lie, I feel bad.

But only a little.

I help myself into the apartment and flop down on her couch. It's not long before she's marching back out of the bathroom with a scowl firmly on her face, still muttering.

Her scowl deepens the moment she spots me. "What the hell are you still doing here?"

"Uh, it's game day."

"And?"

"And I *always* come here on game day."

"Well, I don't want you here. Leave." She points to the door.

"Whoa, whoa, whoa," I say, popping up off the couch. "I can't just leave. I *always* come here on game day."

She rolls her eyes. "Freaking hockey players and their stupid superstitions." She crosses her arms over her chest. "Fine. You can stay, but I am not sleeping with you—not after you just made me piss myself. You can't just walk up and scare pregnant women, Lowell."

"Don't hate on our superstitions, okay? They're a real thing, and there's like lots of science to prove it. Second, I didn't mean to scare you. You left your apartment unlocked, something we should probably really talk about because that is extremely dangerous. I could have been anybody." She opens her mouth to argue, but I keep going anyway. "And third, do you think I just come here for sex?"

"W-Well… Well…" She throws her arms up. "Yes! Isn't that why you come here?"

My mouth falls open in surprise. "Um, no. When have I ever come over here and thrown myself at you or begged for sex? You're the pregnant and horny one, remember?"

"Oh, so you don't want to have sex with me? You're just obliging my request because I'm some sex-crazed maniac, huh?"

"Well, you have the maniac part right."

"Lowell…" she growls.

"Hollis…" I growl back.

She literally huffs and puffs, and I can't help but laugh. She tosses her arms up, trying to walk away from me, but I don't let her. Instead, I pull her into my embrace, wrapping my arms around her.

"Stop, stop, stop," I say, trapping her as I sigh. "I need you to listen to me and listen to me closely here, all right? I am not just here for sex. Do I like it? Yes. Nothing pleases me more than to walk out of this apartment with the smell of you still on my face and fingers." Her eyes darken at my words. "But that's not why I come here. I come here because you're carrying my child and I like spending time with them *and* you. Okay? So don't minimize my coming over here as being just for sex. Though again, I do really love that part."

Like really, really love that part. I probably love that

part way more than I'm supposed to. We've been sleeping together for a while now, and I almost can't remember a time when we weren't sleeping together.

I get it. It's a release for her, and I'm happy to help her out, but I have no idea what that's going to mean for us down the road.

I don't want to think about that or any heavy bullshit right now. It's game day, and I don't come to her apartment on game day to get all up inside my head. I come here to relax.

Also, almost every time I've come here, we've won, but I'm not going to tell her that.

She sighs, then loops her arms around my neck, her fingers going into the edges of my hair, tugging lightly at the strands. "Okay, fine. You can stay."

"I can?"

She nods. "Yes. But, Lowell?"

"Hmm?"

"I changed my mind. I'd really like to have sex now."

"Do it again, but slower."

"Slower?"

"Yeah." She licks her lips as I follow her instructions. "Oh god. Yeah, just like that."

"You like that?"

"I do. I like that *a lot*."

"You want more?"

She traps her lip between her teeth, watching me intently. "Slower."

"I can't go any slower. My jaw is getting cramped already." I wiggle it back and forth, then set my knife down, sitting back in my chair, patting my full stomach. "Plus, I'm stuffed."

"It was one steak!"

"It was one steak two steaks ago, Hollis. I am *full*."

We've been sitting here for the last two hours eating dinner, and since Hollis is not allowed to have rare meat, she's been forcing me to eat the steaks for her.

And by forcing, I mean I definitely wanted to.

"Wimp."

To be fair, the steaks are fairly small, and if I hadn't eaten an entire basket of bread before they arrived, I probably could have finished this one too. What I don't tell Hollis is that I'm trying not to make myself too full because I have a feeling with the way she's been rubbing her thighs together all night, this evening is going to end with both of us naked in her bed.

"Excuse me, waiter, do you think I could get about, oh, twelve ounces of this ranch to go, please?"

Hollis immediately smacks her hand over her mouth, breathing in and out deeply through her nose. I know right away it was just the mention of ranch. I tried to put some on my salad last week and she ran to the bathroom faster than I've ever seen her run—and that includes when I accidentally made her pee her pants...for the second time.

The couple at the table who just asked for the ranch notices.

"Zachary!" the woman seethes. "Stop it!"

"What? This place has really good ranch, and we live like an hour away. There's no way I'm leaving here without some to go."

"Uh, let me go check with my manager." The waiter scurries off, looking as concerned as I am because this guy just ordered an entire small bottle of ranch to go.

The woman jerks her head toward our table. "You just made that woman sick with your disgusting ranch habit."

He gasps. "How dare you! Ranch is not disgusting— you think my ranch habit is cute!"

"Stop saying it!" She glances at Hollis, who is starting to look a little green. "I'm pretty sure she's about a second away from blowing."

Hollis shakes her head up and down, eyes wide, and I laugh, which earns me a glare.

The woman leans over. "I am *so* sorry about him. Sometimes he leaves his manners at home." She glances down at Hollis' round belly. "Oh, you're pregnant! That actually explains so much. You know when my best friend, Zoe, was pregnant, she was the exact same way. Even the mere mention of"—she glances at her husband —"well, the stuff that shall not be named and she was ready to just lose it."

Hollis takes another couple of deep breaths and removes her hand from her mouth. She musters up a small smile. "It's fine. I'm the one who is sorry. I didn't mean to interrupt your meal with my problem."

The woman waves her off. "It's no big deal at all." She turns her eyes on me, squinting. "You look really familiar."

"Delia!" her husband admonishes.

"What?" she asks. "Doesn't he look familiar?"

The guy puts his head in his hands. "That's because you watch him *all the time*. He's the captain for the Carolina Comets, who we're season ticket holders for!"

"Oh!" For a moment she looks embarrassed, then she waves her hand with a shrug. "You know I just go for the snacks and hockey butts. I couldn't tell a first trick from a downtouch or whatever they're called." She sticks her hand out. "Hi, I'm Delia. This is my husband, Zach."

"Hollis." She introduces herself, shaking the woman's hand, then points to me. "And Cam—well, you know him as Lowell."

Zach clears his throat. "Despite my wife not knowing you, I'm a huge fan. I know it's a small world, but you might be a little familiar with my brother. He's an agent for a couple guys on your team. Shep Clark?"

"Ah, yeah. I've met Shep a few times. He reps Rhodes and Wright." Honestly, the dude is a gifted agent and got both of them some pretty sweet deals recently. "Definitely a small world. You said you live an hour away, yeah?"

"Yeah, depending on traffic."

"Have you ever been out to the brewery in Caseyville?"

"We haven't. Driven by lots of times on our way out to Slice." Zach pats his stomach. "That pizza there is killer."

"*So* good. Awful for my waistline in the off-season though. I actually co-own the brewery with my sister."

"No shit? Well, we're definitely stopping in now."

"You should meet up there with Sully and Porter the next time you guys get together to talk apps and security or whatnot," Delia says.

"Apps?"

"Yep," Zach answers. "My company builds them."

"Yeah? My sister mentioned something about wanting to maybe get an app for the brewery. We should get together sometime and talk about that."

Zach's eyes widen. "Dude. I would *love* that. And I won't even ask you to sign my jersey at the meeting."

"You'll just wait until after, right?" Delia asks.

"Obviously."

I laugh. "Deal."

"I hate to cut this short," his wife says, looking at her phone, "but we should head out. Don't want to miss putting the kids to bed."

"You two have kids?" Hollis asks, perking up. "How many?"

She's been doing that often lately. Anytime there's a baby or children around, she pays closer attention to them like she's trying to glean some insight into mothering.

"Eight."

My eyes nearly pop out of my head. "*Eight?*"

She laughs. "Sorry, I should have clarified—our *kids* are goats."

"Pygmy goats to be exact," Zach says, pulling his phone out. "Here, look."

"Are those *Harry Potter* sweaters?"

"Kick-ass, right?"

"Fantastic. The Comets jersey is a nice touch too, but I'm probably a little biased."

Zach laughs, then adds my number to his phone and pockets it. "We'll let you get back to your meal and talk later about the app for the brewery."

"Sounds good."

We shake hands just as the waiter comes back out with a tub of ranch for him. I've never seen someone's face light up so bright before. He cradles it to his chest, and I swear I hear him call it his *precious*.

"Maybe we'll see you at a game?" Delia says as she stands.

Zach slips her jacket around her. "Yeah, you can teach this one that there are no *touchdowns* in hockey."

Hollis laughs. "Don't worry, I am all up to date on the lingo. We'll make you a pro in no time."

She was resistant about learning the game at first, but over the last several months she's really taken a liking to it, and it's something that really turns me on. I like seeing her excited about the game I love so much, and I like seeing her in the stands cheering me on while I play.

Collin and Rhodes have said before that they swear their feet move faster and their sticks hit the puck better when they know Harper and Ryan are in the crowd. I always thought they were full of shit, but I get it now. It's comforting to know there's someone in the stands who doesn't just care about your game, but about you.

It's also great motivation to work hard, because if I play my cards right and we win, I'll score twice that night.

They both wave and turn to leave, but they don't make it far before I hear Zach say to Delia, "I can't believe you didn't recognize him."

"What? He was sitting down. I couldn't see his ass."

Hollis snickers. "They were fun, but when she said eight kids, I about peed myself. I couldn't imagine. I don't even have room for one kid in my apartment, let alone eight." She shakes her head, sipping on her water. "Speaking of…I, uh, found a place that's between the rink and your house."

I sit up taller in my chair, trying not to let my breath sound as shaky as it feels in my chest. "Oh?"

"I—I figured it would be nice to be closer to you for when the baby comes."

"Yeah, uh, I'd, uh, like that."

We sound like scratched-up records, skipping around our words. I especially feel uncomfortable because I have no idea what I'm supposed to say here.

Should I offer to let her move in? Is that what she's hinting at? If not, am I supposed to offer to pay for her apartment? I can afford it, so it's not a big deal, but what's the etiquette here? What is even *here*?

What are we doing? What are—

"Oh, no!" The waiter comes rushing by our table in a panic. "I gave that man blue cheese instead of ranch!"

This time, Hollis does vomit.

Whatever *here* is, we'll have to figure it out later.

CHAPTER 18

HOLLIS

"Oh. My. Gosh!"

My mother's screech is so loud it makes my ears ring.

She wraps her arms around me, pulling me into a hug the best she can since my bump has grown so much. "You look *adorable*, Hollis!"

I force a grin because I sure don't *feel* adorable.

I feel gigantic, exhausted, and just plain overwhelmed all the time. If my feet aren't hurting, it's my back. If I don't have a headache, I'm so tired I can't keep my eyes open. If I'm not hungry, I'm cranky. It has been nonstop one thing after the next, and I am really looking forward to these next few months being over with.

My mother gently cups my protruding belly, and I momentarily feel guilty because I don't even want *her* to touch it.

Just Lowell.

"You're beautiful." She runs her hands over me. "Just beautiful."

"Mom," I whine. "Stop."

"You might as well stop while you're ahead, Mrs. Kelly. She's never going to listen. I try to tell her every day that she's gorgeous, and she always argues with me." Lowell shoots me a look, then sticks his hand out. "It's great to finally meet you. I'm Cameron."

My mother looks down her nose at his hand and then at his face, back to his hand. Finally she slaps it out of the way and pulls him into a giant hug.

"Oh, don't be silly, my dear. Hug me! We're family now!"

It's the first time I've ever heard somebody call Lowell family, and it's the first time I realize he *is* family. Even if Lowell and I aren't together, this baby will always connect us.

That somehow terrifies me and gives me comfort all at once.

My mother shoots me a grin over his shoulder, then winks. *He's cute*, she mouths.

And she's right. He is cute. He's really, *really* cute.

He's cute when he's doing things like rubbing my feet or my belly, fixing me a snack, or grabbing my phone because I forgot to get it before I sat down.

But my favorite part of him? My favorite part of him is at night when he lays his head on my belly and feels our baby move. He does that nearly every night that he's home, actually. I can't remember the last time we've spent a night apart from one another.

That's another thing that somehow terrifies me and gives me comfort all at once. I'm getting so used to him, and I'm starting to worry I'm getting *too* used to him.

We've still yet to discuss the mechanics of what happens after the baby is here. Does he want to move in? Does he want me to move in? Or is he satisfied with what we're doing now? If he's not satisfied with what we're doing now, does he want to co-parent, or will he fight for custody? Will he pay child support, or will he work something else out?

I don't know, and part of me doesn't want to know the answer to any of these questions. I know that's not logical or smart and this is something we need to figure out soon, but not now.

Not now because it's Christmastime and my mom just drove across the state to be here. Though I'll never admit it out loud to her because she'll give me that look that says *I told you so*, I missed my mom and I need her now more than ever.

My mom places her hand on my bump again, then looks at Lowell. "Blink twice if it's a girl."

He doesn't react at all.

He's been very tight-lipped about what we're having, and I love his dedication to it.

"Wait a second—did you just let Mom touch your belly?" Harper asks from the kitchen. "That's bullshit! You *never* let me touch it."

"Really? I touch it all the time," Lowell says.

Harper waves him off. "You don't count, *Dad*."

I don't miss the way he smiles when she calls him

that. I've picked up on how much he enjoys the thought of being a dad, which is exactly why I got him the cheesiest gift I could think of for Christmas, and I can't wait to give it to him.

"Oh, hey, guys," Collin says as he comes padding down the hallway wearing a pair of joggers with the Comets logo on them. "Sorry, I was putting the dogs up. They get a little rambunctious once too many people are here, and I didn't want them bothering anyone."

He wraps his arms around me in a gentle hug.

It's funny because every time I've seen Collin since I told him I'm pregnant, he hugs me, only he always does it lightly like he's terrified he's going to break me by squeezing me too hard.

I know Harper and Collin don't want kids and I completely respect that, but I also know they're going to make the world's greatest aunt and uncle.

"Hey, Col." I squeeze him back just as lightly.

"You're huge," he says, and I *feel* the moment he realizes what he said. He releases me and steps back two feet. "I…I mean… You're…"

Lowell takes an aggressive step toward him, stepping in front of me as if to protect me.

Not going to lie, the move makes me totally wet.

I grab Lowell's shirt, tugging him back. "Down, boy, I know what he meant." I turn to Collin. "I think what you meant to say was, *Gosh, Hollis, that baby sure is growing and you're carrying that extra weight that is definitely not yours so well.*"

He flicks a finger gun at me. "That. That's exactly what I meant."

My mother points to Lowell. "Is this one dumb like this one is?" she asks, referring to Collin.

"Sometimes," I answer honestly.

"Hey!" Lowell objects. "I am not."

"You literally told me *two days ago* that I was 'cute for a pregnant chick.'"

"I didn't… I was…"

Harper walks up and smacks both of them on the back of the head. "Idiots. Both of you."

They both turn red at their moments of idiocy.

The doorbell chimes and Harper grabs Collin, dragging him toward the front door for host duties.

"Come on," she says. "Let's go pretend to be good hosts and greet the rest of your idiot friends."

"They aren't idiots," he argues.

"I beg to differ. I've met Miller."

"Eh." He tips his head back and forth. "Fair."

"So, Lowell," my mother says, grabbing his hand and pulling him toward the kitchen. She hops up on a stool and pats the one next to her, indicating he should sit too. "Tell me, how did you and my daughter meet exactly? She's been very hush-hush on the subject."

My mother and I have been dancing around this subject for months. I know she would never judge me for what happened, but it doesn't make it any less embarrassing that I got pregnant by my one-night stand the night of my sister's wedding. It's even more embarrassing that I punched that one-night stand the day before because I was an emotional wreck.

It's just not something I've wanted to rehash.

"Well, Mrs. Kelly, it's kind of a funny story…" Lowell says, taking a seat next to her.

She slaps at his shoulder. "Oh, stop with that Mrs. Kelly stuff. I'm not much of a Mrs. anymore. My bastard cheating husband has been dead for years."

She says it lightheartedly, but I know what my father did still hurts her, even after all these years. Just like even though I'm pregnant and having a baby with another man, I'm still hurt by what Thad did to me.

Sometimes when I think about everything I've been through in the last six or seven months, it kind of blows my mind. I jumped from one life-changing situation to the next with no room to breathe. No wonder I'm so damn tired all the time.

As if they don't want me to forget about them, the baby moves, and I lay my hand on my belly to calm them.

"Just call me Evelyn," my mother tells him. "Or Nana." She looks at me. "Just no Grandma or Grandmother. I want a cool, fun, young, hip nickname."

"Well, you're not off to a very banging start with that request. Nobody says hip anymore."

"Or cool for that matter."

She waves her hand. "Stop picking on Nana and just tell me the story of how you two met. Don't leave out a single detail either."

Much to my dismay, he doesn't.

Not a single one.

By the time he's finished regaling her with the tale of how we met, everyone—Ryan, Rhodes, Miller, Emilia, and Smith—has arrived for dinner.

My mother stays quiet through the whole thing, not letting out a single peep. Then, when he's finally finished embarrassing me in front of everybody, she looks over at me and says, "Did you throw that punch like your daddy taught you?"

"Yes, ma'am."

She nods once. "Good girl. Now let's eat."

Dinner is finished, most of the mess is cleaned up, and leftovers—what little there are with several hockey players here—are put away. Harper and I are standing side by side at the kitchen sink washing dishes.

Lowell has come in here no less than four times trying to get me to go in there and sit down while he does the dishes, but I keep shoving him out of the kitchen and back to the giant sunroom everyone is crowded in.

"So," Harper starts, bumping her shoulder into mine, "how was your last kid-free Christmas?"

"You mean other than Lowell telling our mother how I punched him?"

She laughs, nodding. "Yes, other than that."

I grin too. "It was nice. Quiet. Even with Miller here."

I scrub my brush over the dirty pan, mulling over what she just asked me. This *was* my last kid-free Christmas, and that's something that didn't even cross my mind until Harper brought it up. I've also now had my last kid-free Halloween and my last kid-free Thanksgiving.

I guess I just never really thought about all the ways those holidays are going to change for me from now on. I wonder if it's something Lowell's thought about.

"How are things going with him?" I glance over at her. "Lowell, I mean. I assume from that dopey grin on your face, that's who you're thinking of."

"It wasn't a dopey grin."

"Oh, it totally was. It's very obvious you two are smitten with each other."

I decide to ignore that. "Things with Lowell are fine. I think we're both starting to really get excited about the baby."

"And is *everything else* fine?" She bounces her brows up and down.

"Very subtle." I laugh. "Everything is…nice."

"Like nice or"—she humps the air—"*nice*?"

I laugh. "The second one."

"Yeah?" She bumps my shoulder again. "Good. I like Lowell."

"I like him too."

"*Like* like him?"

"What is this, middle school?"

"Sometimes it feels like it."

"That's fair. And *like* like. I think."

"You think?"

I shrug. "I don't know. I just got divorced, Harper. It's…well, it's sort of complicated, you know."

She frowns. "Wow. I kind of forgot about that."

"I didn't."

She chuckles. "In that case, just be careful, you know? *Nice* is…well, nice and all, but broken hearts suck."

"So much," I agree. "But I'll be careful."

"Good. Because I'd hate to have to help Collin bury his captain's body." She shakes her head. "I still cannot believe you're having a baby with a hockey player."

"I still cannot believe you're *married* to a hockey player." I wave my hand around the kitchen. "I mean, look at this… Your whole life has changed."

Now she's the one with a dopey grin on her face. "I know. And just think, if I actually had hit him with my car, none of this would have happened."

"It is really concerning how bad at night driving you are."

"It's concerning how bad she is at driving in general," Ryan says, bounding into the room with Emilia and my mother hot on her heels. "One time in college, she ran over her curb so bad she bent the rim and we had to get it towed. But don't worry, she drove on it like that for three days before she had it fixed because she couldn't tell the difference between her bad driving and a bent rim."

My mother's mouth drops open. "Harper Dolores Kelly!"

"I think you mean Harper Dolores *Wright*." My sister grins proudly.

Sometimes with everything crazy that's been going on in my life lately, I forget she and Collin are still firmly in their honeymoon phase.

I try to think back on my honeymoon phase with Thad, but I can't remember a time when I ever looked as happy as Harper looks right now. If I'm being completely honest with myself, whatever is going on with Lowell is probably the happiest I've been in years.

Which is really damn sad when you think about it.

"So, Mother," Harper starts, and the way she says it not-so-nonchalantly has me concerned that I'm not going to like whatever she is about to say. "Now that the guys are in the other room and we can gab without them eavesdropping, what did you think of Lowell?"

I shoot my sister a glare. *Traitor.*

"You mean other than the ass on him?"

"Mother!" I drop the plate I'm holding in the sink, water and bubbles splashing everywhere.

"What? I have eyes, so you can't really blame me. You girls keep bringing around all these hockey players, and everybody knows hockey players have cute butts."

"It's true. I'm pretty sure there was a study done on it or something."

"Yeah. It's just science at this point," Ryan agrees with Emilia.

"I'm like ninety-nine point nine percent sure that's not at all how science works."

"How come nobody knows how science works?" I mutter.

"Anyway," my mother says, ignoring me, "I think he's a catch."

"A catch? Nobody says that anymore."

"First I can't say *cool* or *hip*, and now I can't say *catch*?"

Ryan pats her arm. "Don't worry, Evelyn. My grams is *very* up to date on all the hottest lingo. She can fill you in on what's in these days."

"I would love that. Us grandmothers have to stick together."

I don't tell her Ryan's grandmother is definitely too old for some of the things that come out of her mouth. I've only met her once at Harper and Collin's wedding, and the way that woman was flirting with some of the guys from the team, I was surprised she didn't ask Miller to go home with her. I was also glad, because he might actually have done it.

"Well, since I can't say he's a *catch*, can I say that…" A slow, saccharine grin pulls across her lips. "I like him. I really, *really* like him. And he is going to be an amazing father to your baby, Hollis."

It's probably just the hormones—definitely 100% just the hormones—but my mother's words have tears pooling in my eyes in an instant. I don't think I realized how badly I wanted my mother to approve of the father of my baby.

"Honestly?" She lifts a shoulder. "I'm just glad it's not Thad. That man was a total douchebag. I can still say that, right?"

"Oh my gosh, *thank you*!" Emilia agrees. "I have been saying that for *years*! He gave me such bad vibes."

"He really did. He reminded me of your father, actually."

My mouth slackens. "I had no idea that was how you thought about him, Mom."

"I didn't want to say anything because I knew how much you loved him, and you seemed happy. I thought maybe it was just my own insecurities about my marriage falling apart, and I didn't think it would be fair to put that on your relationship. In the end, it turned out I was right, and that's the last thing I ever wanted." She looks between Harper and me. "I know you girls think I'm overprotective and all I want to do is smother you, and while that may be partially true, I do it because I love you more than anything and I only want what's good for you." She looks pointedly at my belly. "I hope you'll understand that soon too."

I will. I already do.

"I can tell your man out there with the cute butt does."

She winks, and we all laugh, the tension in the room breaking.

"All right, who is in here talking about my cute butt

again?" Collin says as he swaggers into the kitchen, followed closely by the rest of the guys.

"Just because someone mentions a nice butt, doesn't mean they are talking about yours." Harper pats his cheek.

He snorts. "Right. Sure."

"They could be talking about mine." Miller turns around, jutting his backside out for all to see.

"I can assure you, it was not your ass," Emilia deadpans.

I don't miss the way Smith's eyes narrow when Emilia looks at Miller's ass. Much like he did at Harper and Collin's wedding, he catches me staring at him and flicks his gaze away.

Interesting…

"Rude." Miller glares. "I think for that, you owe me a present."

"Is that your way of asking if we can do gifts now?" Harper asks.

He folds his hands under his chin. "Please, Mom?"

She rolls her eyes. "Fine, let's go. Everyone to the big room."

She waves everyone that way, and they all file out until it's just Lowell and me. He wraps his arms around my waist just as I'm drying my hands on the dish towel, and I smile down at the sight, admiring the way his fingers are splayed out over my bump.

"You up for staying around for gifts?" He presses a

kiss into my neck. "I know you weren't feeling well earlier."

My doctor isn't too worried about it as long as I keep hydrated, but I'm still having lots of nausea and am throwing up a few times a week. Parts of me want to hurry this pregnancy along so I don't have to deal with it anymore, but a large part of me wants it to slow down too. It's going too fast, and I admit that I'm a little scared of what's to come next.

"I'm good if you're good."

"I am." I turn in his arms. "Besides, I got you something I think you'll like."

"Oh, are we doing presents?"

Panic shoots through me. *Crap.* I didn't even think to ask. I know we're not *together*, but I just assumed it would be good for me to get the father of my baby a Christmas gift. Is that going too far?

He laughs. "I'm kidding. We're doing presents. You should see your face."

"You're mean." I pinch his sides, and he yelps.

"Hey! Be nice. Coach will have your ass if you go damaging this body."

"I'm not scared of Coach."

"You should be. He's little but mean."

"I'm little but mean."

"True, but you won't hurt me."

"Yeah?"

"Nah. I'm too much of a *catch* for you to do that."

I gasp. "You heard that?"

"I will neither confirm nor deny that all of us guys were standing around the corner listening in."

"Cameron!" I hiss. "That's awful!"

He shrugs. "It's good for our ego."

"Yeah, because everyone's talking about your nice butts."

"I don't hear you complaining about my nice butt."

"Eh. It's okay."

"Okay?" He looks offended. "Just *okay*?"

"Yep." I grab his hand, tugging him toward where I can already hear Miller getting into the gifts. "Now come on. Let's open presents so we can go home and you can touch *my* butt."

His brows rise. "Like really, *really* touch your butt?"

"Depends on how fast we get these gifts opened."

Then he's the one tugging *me* out of the room.

CHAPTER 19

They say absence makes the heart grow fonder. I don't know who the fuck *they* were, but they were right.

We are currently on a six-game road trip with a four-game losing streak. I miss my bed. I miss Hollis' bed. I miss having Hollis *near* me in my bed.

But most of all? Most of all I miss our baby.

"Well, that was a shit show." Collin drops onto the bench next to me, popping his gear off with all the frustration I feel too. "We fucking sucked out there."

I'm supposed to be the team captain. I'm supposed to come back with the rally in response and get us motivated to get out of this slump, supposed to get us ready and get us out there to win the next game.

But right now, I agree. We fucking sucked out there. We knew it. The crowd knew it. The other team knew it. *Everybody* knew it. We were not playing like the Cup-winning champions I know we can be, and it was frustratingly embarrassing.

I wish we were at home right now. If I'm playing shit

hockey, I'd rather play shit hockey at home so at least I can go back home to Hollis.

We need to get our heads out of our asses and get those points back. We're at too crucial of a point in the season to be letting everything slip away like this.

"Fuck," Miller groans, plopping down on the other side of me. "How is it we played that bad and I'm this tired?"

I shrug. "Being away from home sucks."

"You got that right. I don't know how you guys do it, being away from your women all the time." He bumps his shoulder against mine. "Pretty soon you'll be away from your woman *and* your kid."

"She's not my woman."

He sends me an incredulous look. "Dude, pretty sure she's your woman. You're having a kid with her."

"So?"

"So, that makes her *yours*."

"Nah. People co-parent all the time."

"Yeah, but do other people sleep together *and* co-parent? Oh, wait. That's not called co-parenting—that's called a *relationship*," Rhodes says from across the room, lifting a brow.

"Hey, now," Collin chimes in. "Don't go saying the R-word around Lowell. We all know he'll run and hide."

I look across the way to Smith, expecting him to back me up, but I don't find a sympathetic look on his face. If anything, he looks like he agrees with the Three Stooges over here.

It annoys me that he agrees. Out of everybody in this room, Smith should know how I feel. He's been married to the game longer than I have. Hell, he's the one who *taught* me to shut my feelings off and just play.

That's what I'm doing. I'm shutting down and shutting out everything else. I'm playing—albeit horribly —but I'm focusing on hockey and the baby. I'm not thinking about Hollis or how she has the power to crush my heart. I'm not thinking about that at all.

"Shut up," I grumble to all of them. "Get dressed. We have a plane to catch."

"Oooh, someone's eager to get home to *his* woman," Miller taunts.

"I just want you to know, Miller, when he clocks you, I'm going to laugh and laugh and laugh," Rhodes says.

"I will also laugh. And possibly hold you down."

"Hey!" Miller shoots daggers at Collin. "What did I ever do to you?"

"Exist."

"Is this a normal occurrence in your life?" Miller leans into me, keeping his voice low as he stares out at the scene in front of us. "Because this is kind of making me uncomfortable."

I know what he means. I get uncomfortable dealing with it too.

"Yeah. Happens a few times a week. But…" I lift a shoulder. "It's worth it. I hope."

Hollis is currently holding up a baby outfit that has giraffes on it and sobbing. It's the crying that's making Miller uncomfortable.

He grins. "Yeah, it's worth it. I never thought I'd be into pregnant chicks, but Hollis looks hot all knocked up."

I turn toward him with a glare that has him cowering back and holding his hands up.

"Hey, now…I didn't mean anything by it. I just m-meant that, uh, um…"

"Miller?" I clench and unclench my fists, trying to talk myself out of punching the guy at our baby shower.

"Yeah?"

"Go. Away."

"Roger that."

He runs away faster than I've ever seen him move on the ice, and that's saying something because the kid is fast as fuck on skates.

"Those are some rather territorial vibes you're giving off about somebody you're not even dating." Smith sidles up next to me, a glass of whiskey in his hand. "Because you're allegedly still not dating, right?"

I ignore him, staring back out at Hollis, watching as she tosses her head back and laughs, wiping away her tears. Harper and Emilia are sitting on either side of her, Ryan on the floor with a pad of paper in her lap, jotting down notes for thank-you cards later.

My house isn't sprawling big or anything, but I have a lot of room, especially compared to Hollis' apartment. Though with the mountain of gifts surrounding her, I have no idea where I'm going to put it all.

Even though our schedule is exhausting and I'm pretty sure they'd all rather be somewhere else on their off day, the team showed up to support us in droves. Nearly every single member from our roster is here, and Coach Heller is over in the corner enjoying the finger foods with his wife. Hell, even our goalie, who is notorious for not liking kids, is here.

Not that I would ever admit it to any of these bastards, but it feels good to know they care about us enough to be here today. I know Hollis appreciates the support too.

She looks at me from across the room, and her face lights up the moment our eyes connect. She looks happy, so damn happy. It's such a shift from the mascara-stained crazy woman I met last summer.

Craziest part is I'd take her both ways.

"Come on, man. You can't really tell me you're not dating—not when you're looking at her like that."

"I don't know what you're talking about. There's nothing going on."

It's a lie.

We both know it's a lie.

I hate that we both know it just as much as I hate the look he's giving me right now.

"Uh-huh. Sure. Right. Nothing at all."

"What's going on with you and Emilia? Is that nothing too?" I shoot back, and he snaps his mouth closed, looking a whole lot less cocky. I smirk. "That's what I thought."

"Nothing is going on with me and"—he swallows thickly—"her."

I scoff. "You can't even say her name."

"I can too."

"Prove it."

He tips his chin up. "No. I don't need to prove shit to you."

"Weird. I don't need to prove shit to you either."

I shove past him, retreating into the kitchen for something, *anything* to get me away from him and his curious stare.

I open the fridge and look around, but I have no idea what I'm looking for. The baby shower was catered, and there's nothing in here I could possibly take out there that's going to make any sense.

"Are you hiding?"

In so many ways.

I turn around to find Hollis standing just inside the kitchen, her hand resting on her very pregnant belly.

The sunlight is poking in behind her, radiating around her like the beacon of light in a dark stormy night that she is. She's gorgeous, and the urge to kiss her and touch her overpowers me.

I cross the open kitchen, grabbing her hand and dragging her down the hallway to my bedroom. I don't stop until we're inside and I have her back pressed against the door.

She gasps and blinks up at me with surprise when I press my erection into her.

"I'm not hiding. *We're* hiding."

"We are?"

"Yes, and I can't believe you just dragged me in here to ravish me, you little minx."

She grins. "Oh, I did?"

"Yes, you did." I run my nose along her cheek. "And then you instructed me to push this entirely too sexy dress up and get on my knees so I can see your pretty cunt."

She lets out a soft moan, and I haven't even done anything to her yet.

"Lowell…we have guests."

"So? They can wait. Besides, I'll be quick." I wink.

I sink to my knees, grab the hem of her dress, and lift. She has to adjust herself when the dress gets to her belly, and she sighs in frustration.

"Ugh. I'm so…"

I stop, looking up at her with a sharp stare. "I *know* you weren't just about to say something disparaging about your body, Hollis."

She shakes her head. "N-No."

"Are you lying to me?"

"Depends. Will I get punished if I am?"

I start to push to my feet, and she quickly shoves me back down.

"Fine! Yes, I was going to say something about my…*situation*. You happy?"

"No."

I hook my fingers into her panties, then drag them down her legs. I grab one leg and haul it over my shoulder, loving the way she shivers when the cool air hits her exposed pussy.

"One compliment, one lick."

"Huh?"

I look up at her. "You say one compliment about yourself, and this beautiful pink cunt of yours gets one lick."

"O-One lick? It'll take more than that."

"Then keep talking."

"I…I don't have anything to say. I—"

I go to push to my feet again, and she lets out a little squeak.

"I'm beautiful!" she shouts out, and I grin at the urgency in her voice.

I swipe my tongue over her, and she sighs. I pull away, and she whimpers.

"Keep going," I encourage.

"I…I'm…I'm gorgeous."

Another swipe.

"I'm adorable."

Another taste.

"I'm cute."

Another lick.

"I'm sexy."

Another stroke.

"I'm *yours*."

Mine.

I suck her clit into my mouth, and she cries out, her fingers tangling in my hair, playing with the strands as I get lost in the taste of her. I suck and kiss and eat, fucking her with my fingers and tongue, and I don't let up until her legs are shaking and I'm practically holding her up.

"Please, Cameron. *Please.*"

I rub that spot inside of her I know she likes and suck on her clit until she explodes, her body going stiff for a moment before coming down from her high. I sit back, admiring my work as she leans against the door, her legs still shaky and her breaths even shakier.

We don't talk as I slip her panties back up her legs and right her dress before wiping my face and leading us back out to the party. In fact, we don't utter a word all day until we lie down that night and slip between my sheets, where we use our bodies to speak all the words we could never say.

CHAPTER 20

Lowell: Gordie?

Hollis: Umm…no.

Lowell: Howe?

Hollis: How what?

Lowell: No. Like Gordie Howe.

Hollis: Goldie Hawn???

Lowell: What? NO!

. . .

Lowell: GORDIE HOWE

Hollis: Never heard of her.

Lowell: I…

Lowell: I thought your hockey knowledge was much more up to par than this.

Lowell: I have failed you.

Lowell: In fact, I'm retiring right now. I cannot, in good conscience, have a baby with a woman who doesn't know who Gordie Howe is.

Hollis: You'll get over it.

Lowell: Sorry. I can't come to the phone right now. I'm dead.

. . .

Hollis: And dramatic. Don't forget dramatic.

Hollis: Um...sir?

Lowell: Okay, first, I didn't realize that would be hot.

Hollis: It's not happening, so move on.

Lowell: *grumbles* Fine. Moving on.

Lowell: How may I help you, ma'am?

Hollis: Did you have a pizza delivered to my apartment? Specifically a heart-shaped one?

Lowell: Oh. That.

Lowell: Yeah, it was me.

. . .

Hollis: Why????

Lowell: Because it's Valentine's Day.

Lowell: Our baby might not be here yet, but I wanted to make sure Momma was taken care of.

Hollis: That's…really sweet. Like really, really sweet.

Hollis: I kind of want to kiss you right now.

Lowell: I'd let you.

Hollis: I'm sure you would.

Lowell: I wish we weren't on the road AGAIN.

Lowell: Fuck, I hate road games.

· · ·

Lowell: Especially because I'm always stuck on the bus next to Miller and he never wants to shut the hell up.

Hollis: Miller shuts up?

Lowell: No. Literally never.

Lowell: Right now, he's telling me the same story he started telling me ON THE PLANE.

Lowell: That was HOURS ago.

Lowell: And it's not even a good story. I guessed the ending two minutes into it.

Hollis: Tell him to pipe down.

Lowell: I have. I do.

Lowell: Next time, I'm bringing duct tape.

· · ·

Hollis: He'll probably just lick it off.

Lowell: Probably.

Lowell: How's work going? Getting ahead like you wanted to?

Hollis: Yes, though I think I'm going to call it a night. I'm tired. Baby is sucking up all my energy today.

Lowell: Go rest, then. Take your pizza to bed and spoon with it and pretend it's me.

Hollis: That's not weird at all.

Lowell: Hey, I know some people who take their pizza very seriously and wouldn't bat an eye.

Hollis: I am really scared to know if you're "some people."

. . .

Lowell: Guess you'll never know.

Hollis: See you tomorrow?

Lowell: Yes.

Lowell: Oh, and happy Valentine's Day.

Lowell: I'll give you your present tomorrow. *tongue emoji*

Lowell: Elsa?

Hollis: She's a total badass, but no.

Hollis: What about Georgia?

Lowell: Like the state?

. . .

Hollis: Yes.

Lowell: Hmm…I don't hate it.

Hollis: This would be a lot easier if I knew what we were having…

Lowell: It would be, except you don't want to know, remember?

Lowell: In fact, you promised me bodily harm if I tried to tell you.

Hollis: So you're saying you're scared of me?

Lowell: HA! Not a chance.

Lowell: But also…yes.

Lowell: Then again, if you punched me, it wouldn't be the first time.

. . .

Hollis: LOWELL!

Hollis: I swear, if you keep bringing that up…

Lowell: It was traumatic!

Hollis: It was not! If anything, it probably turned you on.

Hollis: Lowell?

Hollis: Oh god.

Hollis: It did, didn't it??

Hollis: LOWELL!

Hollis: Oh, wait. I just realized you're probably playing hockey right now.

. . .

Hollis: GO TEAM! TOUCHDOWN!

Hollis: I think the doctor missed flirting with you today.

Lowell: I'm sorry I couldn't be there.

Hollis: Me too.

Lowell: How'd it go?

Hollis: Everything is looking good. Baby is healthy.

Lowell: And Momma?

Hollis: She's healthy too. Just hungry.

Lowell: What do you want? I'll send you food.

. . .

Hollis: You don't have to send me food every time I'm hungry. I'm a big girl. I can feed myself.

Hollis: Besides, I have another appointment to get to.

Lowell: Another one?

Lowell: I don't see anything on my Google calendar.

Hollis: It's for an apartment viewing.

Lowell: Oh.

Lowell: Is that what you want? A bigger apartment?

Hollis: More like I NEED a bigger one.

Hollis: Hell, YOU barely fit in this one.

· · ·

Hollis: Besides, it'll be nice to be closer to you and the rink and everything. Makes it easier on everyone for when the baby comes.

Lowell: Because you'll be there, and I'll be here.

Hollis: Exactly.

Lowell: That is what you want, right?

Hollis: Are you coming over tonight?

Lowell: Probably not. Early morning at the rink. Rain check?

Hollis: Sure.

Lowell: Night.

CHAPTER 21

HOLLIS

"Oh shit," I groan, sitting up on the couch where I fell asleep watching Lowell's hockey game.

I rub a hand across my forehead, a dull throb beginning. I feel like I've been run over, but I assume that's because I didn't sleep well last night alone in my bed. I spent way too much time thinking and tossing and turning and not enough time sleeping.

I place a hand on my belly, trying to soothe the slight cramps I'm having, my stomach clearly not agreeing at all with the burrito I had for lunch. I check the score on the game and see that the Comets are losing with just seven to go in the third, and if they lose, Lowell is going to be in a mood when he comes over.

If he comes over.

He hasn't for the last few nights, which is not like him at all. In fact, I can't remember the last time we didn't spend the night together when he's had a home game. Not having him in my bed feels wrong, like so wrong it makes my stomach hurt. Or maybe that's the burrito.

The worst part is, I don't know whether it's something I did wrong or if he's feeling wrong about something we're doing, but neither option sits right with me.

My stomach cramps again, and I wince at the pain.

"Sorry about that, baby. Momma promises not to get burritos from that food truck ever again."

I wonder if it *was* the burrito though, because I didn't feel all that great yesterday either.

"How about this? If Momma isn't feeling better in the morning, she'll call the doctor, okay?"

The baby kicks as if they agree, and I grin.

The first time I felt a flutter, I cried. Lowell was sleeping next to me, and I cried so hard I woke him up with my sobs. Then we stayed up until two AM just feeling our baby move.

The movements are *a lot* more than just a flutter now, and I'm almost positive these little moments between us are what I'm going to miss most about being pregnant.

I keep my hand on my belly and turn my attention back to the game. The time starts to move fast on the clock, and the Comets are still down a goal. There are only three minutes left now, and they pull their goalie.

I know this can always be a huge gamble to take. They can either make up the point they're missing, or they're giving the other team a chance to score an empty-netter and seal the deal.

Unfortunately, favor is not with them tonight, because not even ten seconds into the man advantage, the other team sends the puck flying down the ice and right into the empty net. The camera operator zooms in on Lowell's face on the bench, and he looks completely defeated and disappointed. I know how bad they need these points tonight, but the chances are looking slim right now.

Another bad cramp hits me, and I'm almost starting to wonder if this is more than I think it is.

I push off the couch to head into the bathroom, and the moment I do, I *know* this *is* more than I think it is. The room feels all wobbly and wonky and off, and I feel like I might pass out. I collapse back onto the couch, trying to catch my breath. My head begins to throb, and I feel like there are a thousand little elephants dancing inside of it.

Something is wrong.

I reach for my phone and begin to call Lowell, then remember he's in the middle of a game. He can't answer or do anything about it.

Instead, I dial Harper.

She answers almost immediately.

"Please tell me you are watching this game. This is miserable. They need these points *so* badly. Collin is going to be so upset when he gets home. I—"

"Harper," I cut her off sharply.

"What's wrong?" she says, and I can already hear the panic setting into her voice. It's the same panic that's setting into me too. "Is something wrong? Is everything okay?"

"I need you to take me to the hospital."

I hear Lowell before I see him.

"Where the fuck is she?" he growls, and I feel bad for whichever nurse he's snarling at right now. "Where is Hollis?"

Not even five seconds later, he comes barreling into the tiny room I'm in.

His eyes are wide as he takes me in all hooked up to the machines, his lips set with worry as he rushes toward me. He just stands there and stares and stares and stares some more. His eyes are glassy and panicked, and his breaths are coming in sharp.

Then everything snaps back to reality for him, and he crosses the room, taking my face in his hands.

"Is the baby okay?"

He runs his hands over my cheeks and through my hair, looking me over for any signs of damage. There are none; it's all internal.

I love that the first thing out of his mouth is about the baby.

"The baby is fine," I promise him. "Just a little scare."

He sags against me in relief, pressing a hard kiss to my forehead. "What happened? Harper didn't tell me anything, just said I needed to get here. I came straight after the game."

"Harper can be so dramatic."

"Dramatic?" He nods toward all the stuff I'm hooked up to. "Then what's all this?"

"Monitors for me and the baby. I also had to pee in a cup, which is very hard when you're this pregnant. And they checked my cervix, which was almost more painful than the reason I came in."

"And that was for?"

"I felt a little lightheaded and had a bad headache, some cramps."

"Cramps? Like Braxton Hicks?"

"You know what Braxton Hicks are?"

"What?" He shrugs. "I read."

I grin. "It wasn't Braxton Hicks. These were different. Just…uncomfortable. I was a little dehydrated."

He pulls back and tips his head. "Dehydrated? Like you're not drinking enough water?"

"I thought I was. I've been peeing enough that it feels like I am."

His brows are drawn tightly together as he steps away from me, and it's a good thing because I do *not* like the look he's giving me right now. "Hollis, you pee *all* the time, even when you shouldn't be peeing. You have a baby pressing down on your bladder. That doesn't mean you're drinking enough."

"I-I'm sorry. I thought…"

He shakes his head. "It's not just you, Hollis. This is about my baby too."

I whip my head back at his words, surprised. I have no idea where his sudden hostility and frustration is coming from, but I know I don't deserve it. The baby is okay, and that's all that matters.

"*Our* baby."

"You know what I mean."

I glare at him. "No, sorry. I don't."

"It's reckless of you to not—"

"Reckless? *Reckless?* You act like I did this on purpose! I've been sick, Lowell! It's not my fault."

"Sick?"

"Yes! And you'd know that if you were around."

"Oh god." He rolls his eyes. "Excuse me if I've been busy playing *hockey*. You know I can't always be around during the season."

"You've had no problems with it until recently."

"What's that supposed to mean?"

"It means, in case you haven't noticed, you haven't exactly been around lately."

He hasn't. Not for days. He hasn't come over. He's barely texted me. He's been pulling away whether he's ready to admit it or not.

"I've been playing hockey! In the NHL!"

"Stop saying that! Stop saying that like it matters or changes anything. Every other night this season you've had no problem spending the night in my bed."

"Is that what this is?" He scoffs, pacing back and forth with a look of disgust lining his features. "You're mad because I haven't been around to *fuck* you?"

The air is sucked out of my lungs at his words, and I swear if I wasn't all hooked up, I would be out of this bed and out of this room so fast because I cannot stand to be in it with him for another minute.

I have no idea who I'm looking at right now. Whoever it is, it's not Lowell.

This isn't the same man who has spent countless nights rubbing my back or helping me up to pee in the middle of the night. This isn't the same man who had a heart-shaped pizza delivered to me just a few weeks ago because he was worried I wasn't eating enough. This isn't the same man who looks at me like I'm the only person in the world. This isn't the same man who looks *at* me, especially not when he's staring through me right now.

This man? This isn't the man who makes me feel like I'm his.

I don't know this man, and I don't want to know him either.

"I—"

The door is pushed open, and I snap my mouth shut, not wanting to argue with Lowell in front of the doctor.

She beams at us, walking farther into the room. "Ah! Your husband is here. That's—"

"We're not together. I'm just the dad."

My heart drops, and I know if I were standing up right now, I'd need to sit down.

His words are harsh and final, and even though I know we never defined just what it is we're doing, I didn't expect it to feel like I'm having my heart ripped out of my chest at the way he *insists* we're nothing.

I'm not asking for a ring or a commitment, but does

what we've spent the past several months doing really mean nothing to him?

Because it means something to me.

By the tone in his voice, it means *too* much to me.

Lowell isn't looking at me. He's only staring at the doctor, who is shifting her eyes between the two of us.

"Well?" Lowell prompts, lips flattened in a frown.

The doctor clears her throat. "You're being released, *Miss* Kelly. Everything is looking much better now. Just need to make sure you're drinking lots of fluids." She turns to Lowell. "Maybe grab a sports drink or two on the way home, Mr. Lowell. As an athlete, I'm sure you're aware of the benefits of replenishing your electrolytes." She turns back to me. "Sound good? Any questions for me before we get you discharged?"

"No, Dr. Kane, thank you so much for your help today. I really appreciate it."

She smiles. "It's no problem at all. We see this happen from time to time, especially when the mother-to-be is under stress. Just make sure you're resting, taking breaks when you can, and trying to avoid any stress triggers. It can make that mommy brain even worse." She winks. "I'll get these to the front desk, and we'll get you on your way shortly."

She shuffles out of the room, leaving us to slowly die in this oxygen-deprived space.

"Is that what you want, Lowell?"

He snaps his eyes up. "Huh?"

"When the baby comes…is that what you want to be? Just the dad?"

He knows what I'm asking.

He knows what I'm asking, and he just stands there. He doesn't answer. Just stares at me…*through* me.

I hate it so much.

And in this moment, I hate *him* so much.

"I—"

"Pardon me, Mr. Lowell, but we wanted to go over some insurance information with you."

He clamps his mouth shut, sending me one last glance before following the doctor out of the room, and I have my answer.

I'm not alone long enough to let the reality of what just happened simmer before a nurse comes in and helps get me unhooked and out of bed. She's dropping me into a wheelchair—hospital policy—when she asks, "Do you have someone to take you home?"

"They'll be waiting outside."

She nods, then wheels me through to the front entrance. She's helping me out of the wheelchair and into the car when Lowell comes skidding out of the sliding glass door of the hospital.

"Hollis, wait!" he calls out, jogging down the sidewalk to us.

"Thanks," I say to the nurse. "We got it from here."

She glances from me to Lowell, making sure I'm good, then takes the wheelchair and leaves.

"You can't be serious," Lowell says, coming to a stop before me. "You're leaving with Harper?"

"What does it matter to you who I leave with, Lowell? *We're not together*, remember?"

He opens his mouth to say something, then snaps it closed. He knows they're his words I'm hurling back at him, which is why he can't even defend himself right now.

"I'll text you." And I will. I'm pregnant with his baby. I'm not shutting him out. I turn to Harper, who is shooting a nasty look Lowell's way. "Let's go."

She helps me into her car, glaring at him the entire time. When we're about to pull away, she sighs, and I know she's about to dive into the *I told you so* speech.

"Don't," I say to her quietly. "Please. Not now."

Another sigh, then a nod.

I watch Lowell disappear in the rearview mirror, leaving half of my heart in the hospital parking lot.

CHAPTER 22

I can't even begin to count the number of times I've been hurt in all my years of playing hockey. I've had broken bones. I've taken one-hundred-plus-mile-per-hour pucks in places people should never take pucks. I've lost teeth. I've been beaten to the point of being unable to walk for days.

I've played through it all.

But this hurt? I'm not sure I can handle it.

And this time, it's all my fault.

I fucked up.

I fucked up *big*, and not just out on the ice where we blew a three-to-one lead yesterday and lost seven to three because my head was completely out of the game.

No. I fucked up long before tonight, so many times in fact.

I should have never kissed Hollis.

I should have never slept with her.

I should have never *kept* sleeping with her.

And I definitely, one hundred percent should not have fallen in love with her.

But I did, I did, I did, and I *so fucking did*.

Standing in that hospital room seeing her with all those straps and monitors on her broke me. It broke me and it fucking scared me that it broke me, because this isn't about us. It was never supposed to be about us.

Things with Hollis were never supposed to be this serious. One time, one night, and we move on. One night and we act like it never happened. She wasn't supposed to still be around, and she definitely wasn't supposed to get pregnant.

This whole thing has been a mess from the beginning, and I only have myself to blame for giving in to the temptation and breaking my rule that hockey comes first no matter what. I don't know the exact moment I fell for her—probably when she punched me—but I know the exact moment I realized I couldn't love her. I can't love her because if I do, I can lose her. If I never love her at all, I'll never know what it feels like to lose her, and I can walk away intact.

But that's bullshit.

It's always been bullshit.

I know that now. I know that because I'm sitting on this godforsaken bench in a million shattered pieces, and I have no clue how to put myself back together.

"How do you want it?"

I sigh, because I knew I'd be hearing from him at some point. I finish lacing up my skates, then look at

Collin, who is standing over me with his arms crossed and a murderous stare etched into his eyes.

He's pissed, and I don't blame him one bit.

I sit back, meeting his ire because I deserve it and I know I do.

"How do I want what?"

"Your death. Poisoning? Axe? Arrow? Shovel? Rope? Knife? Chainsaw? Spoon? Take your pick."

"Fuck off. I'm not in the mood for your games."

"Oh, trust me—this isn't a game."

Imagine my fucking surprise when he actually pulls a spoon out of his back pocket and whacks me on top of the head with it.

"OW! What the…"

He grabs me by the sweater, pulling me off the bench and tugging me until we're nearly touching noses.

"Fuck off, Wright," I seethe, ignoring the surprised cries of *What the fuck* from our teammates, who are already half-dressed getting ready for practice. "It's not your battle."

"Bullshit it's not. Your girl has been on my couch for the last week while my girl is fixing her. It's my problem as much as it's yours."

He pulls me close until we're nose to nose, and I grab his sweater, shoving at him, but he doesn't budge. "Leave it alone."

"No!" he roars.

I shove him again, catching his chin with my fist that's holding his sweater. It's the first hit, and it's all it takes for his eyes to darken and for him to take a swing at me.

I let him hit me. I let him hit me because I deserve it and so much more.

I don't know how long he hits me. I stop counting, and I stop hitting back. I just take it, accepting my punishment.

Because this? What's happening right now? It's nothing compared to how I'm feeling on the inside.

"Dude, dude. Whoa. Come on, man, that's enough, all right? Chill out."

Rhodes pulls on him, trying to drag him away. He doesn't relent, and I like that he doesn't relent. I like that he's here having Hollis' back. I've never been happier to be hit in my entire life.

"What the fuck is going on in here?!"

Collin drops me the instant Coach blazes into the room, a glower marring his face as he takes in the sad state of each of us. His hands are on his hips, his lips pressed and angry. He shakes his head, looking completely disgusted by both of us.

"Is this what we're doing now, huh? Fighting each other instead of the other team?" He scoffs. "Fucking despicable." He points a finger at Collin. "Scratched, starting tonight." Then he points to me. "You? *Two* games. You're supposed to be leading this team, especially right now when we need it the most. Instead, you're in here fighting with your own teammates. You know better than that, *Captain*."

I hate the way he spits the word at me.

I don't feel like a captain. Especially not right now.

I nod, accepting it.

"Good. Now get the fuck out on that ice and leave whatever this bullshit is in here. Understood?" He laughs derisively, shaking his head and muttering as he walks out. "Fuckin' children. All a bunch of children."

The door slams shut behind him and the room is completely quiet, everyone just watching to see what's going to happen next between Collin and me.

We stare each other down for a long time until finally, Rhodes lays a hand on his shoulder.

"We got practice, man. This is over."

"It's not. It's not over. He doesn't get to just break her and walk away. That's not how it works."

"Break *her*?" I mutter. "I didn't break her. She broke me."

Collin whirls back around, ready for more. "What'd you say?"

"I said I didn't break Hollis. *She* broke *me*, and I love her, okay?" I shove myself up, staggering just slightly from being knocked around like a punching bag. I rub at my jaw that's already throbbing, trying to catch my breath that just won't seem to come. "I love her. Are you fucking happy now?"

"No," Collin seethes. "I won't be happy until she's happy, and you have a lot of fucking fixing to do."

"This is all your fault," I say to Smith as we head into the building for the game tonight—the game I *won't* be playing in because I'm a healthy scratch.

Everyone knows that's the worst kind of scratch to be. It means you've screwed up and now you have to pay by forcing your team to pick up the slack without you while you sit in the box with the night off, watching the repercussions of your actions.

It fucking sucks, and it especially blows because Coach wants Collin and me up in the box together. Based on the bruises on my face and the split lip he's rocking, it's clear we got into it with one another. The press is going to have a fucking field day with it no doubt.

"Yeah? And how's that exactly?"

"You told me to ask her to dance, and I did. If I hadn't, I wouldn't be in this mess at all."

His brows rise, and I hate that the look he's giving me says we both know that's not true. I think even if Hollis and I hadn't danced that night, we would have still ended up in that garden together, wrapped around one another like a clandestine meeting under the stars.

If we hadn't, Smith would have told me to ask her to dance.

He knew all along.

Fucker.

"What are you going to do?"

I look back at Fiona. The only thing I want to do is jump inside of her and drive to Hollis and tell her how sorry I am.

But I can't. I have to be here, for a hockey game I'm not even fucking playing in because Coach is sadistic.

"I'm going to fix it. Eventually."

"How?"

"I don't know."

"This might sound fucking nuts, but have you tried honest communication?"

I snort. "Like you've tried with Emilia?"

"My situation is a little more…complicated."

"And mine isn't?"

"No. It's pretty straightforward if you just get your head out of your ass and look at it from a non-damaged perspective."

"But I *am* damaged."

He stops walking, turning to me. "You're right. You are—but so is Hollis. She got divorced less than a year ago because her husband was *cheating* on her. Then she got pregnant right after. She's damaged too, but guess what? She's not going around putting up walls and blocking people out because she's afraid. She's facing this shit head-on, which is a lot more than I can say for you."

I…*fuck*. He's right. I *know* he's right.

"I know." I scrub a hand over my face, exhaling sharply. "I know, okay? I'm an idiot. A bigger idiot than Miller."

"Yeah, you are," Miller says as he walks by shooting me judgy eyes.

Shit. Even the rookie is on my case.

Smith sighs. "I've put my life on hold for my career.

I've been married to this game for longer than you've been alive. Hockey is my life, but it doesn't have to be yours. So, if you love her and there's a chance for you to have a family, take that chance. Because trust me, Lowell, these years? They're going to fly by fast, and before you know it, you'll be an old man like me signing one-year contracts hoping you can hold on to the game you love for just a little longer because you know when it's over, you'll truly be alone."

I swallow, my mouth sticky and dry just thinking about living a life without Hollis in it. I mean, yeah, we'll always be connected because of the baby, but just thinking of another man raising my child too, another man touching her…knowing her the way I do…

I can't stomach it.

It's supposed to be me.

I'm yours, she promised.

Mine, I swore.

"Tell her, Lowell."

CHAPTER 23

HOLLIS

"All right, tell me what's going on."

My brows scrunch together. "I don't know what you mean. Nothing's going on."

Emilia looks at me with shrewd eyes. "Hmm, nice try. But you're my best friend and I know you better than that. So, tell me…what happened?"

Everything happened.

"It was…nothing."

"It wasn't *nothing*. You were dehydrated and in the hospital, so it clearly wasn't nothing."

Oh. That's what she's talking about.

"Right. It was just that—a little dehydration, but I'm better now."

"Good. I'm glad. Now tell me about what happened with Lowell."

My heart leaps into my throat just hearing his name. "W-What about him?"

"Why is he moping around the rink?"

He is?

I think in another life at another time, it would give me a bit of satisfaction to know he's hurting like I'm hurting.

But it doesn't. If anything, it makes me feel worse.

A small wave of discomfort surges through my belly, and I rub it to help soothe it. I take a mental note of the time like I have been all day since they began in the wee hours of the morning. They're getting closer together and more painful, that's for sure.

"I don't know what you mean," I say to her, pushing through the discomfort.

"Yes, you do. Start talking."

I know she's not going to give up. To be fair, I knew she wasn't going to give up when she came over here tonight when she's supposed to be working. She took a personal day just to spend time with me. I love her for it, but I also would have been fine having a night to myself to sulk.

I finally convinced Harper to stop "dropping by" to check on me, to not swoop me out of my apartment for a "girls' day" and kidnap me to take me to her house and watch the game tonight, which Collin is back in action for after being a healthy scratch last night.

I was at their house when he came back from practice with a busted lip. I didn't ask how he got it. I already knew.

It made me love that Collin is going to be my baby's uncle just a little more in that moment. I know they'll always be safe with him around.

I fill Emilia in on everything. What happened at the hospital, what happened before that. Everything that's been running through my mind for the last several months.

When I'm finished, she doesn't say anything for several long moments. Then, her lips pull into a soft smile, the bun of beautiful red hair piled up high tipping sideways with her head tilt. "You love him, don't you?"

I sink my teeth into my bottom lip. "I do. But that's bad, right? I…I just got out of a long-term relationship. Hell, out of a marriage. I can't be in love with someone else already, can I?"

"Of course you can. There's no timeline on things like this, Hollis. Is that what's been holding you back?"

In a way, it is. I didn't tell Harper that because, no offense to her, she wouldn't understand. She doesn't know what it's like to promise yourself to someone and have them betray you in the worst way possible.

Emilia…she understands.

"Yes. No. I don't know. We never officially defined what we were, you know? We just…*were*. Until we weren't."

"But it felt like you were dating, didn't it?"

I nod. "Yes."

As much as I told myself not to, I got attached to him. I got attached to us.

"When the doctor came into the room and called him my husband…" I trail off, conjuring up the image of

273

the look on his face when she said that with ease. "He said he was *just the dad*. That was it."

I can't stop thinking about the way he looked at me in that hospital room. He looked angry and scared and hurt and back to scared. I get it—I was scared too.

But it was more than that with him. He looked unsure. About us…about everything.

That scared me more than anything else. I can't open my heart to someone again and then get hurt. I just can't. I have more than me to think about. I have my baby too.

"I see the wheels turning in your head, and you're a fool if you think that man doesn't love you, Hollis. I've seen the way he looks at you. You mean the world to him. I'd wager to bet you mean *more* than the world to him. He won't hurt you. I know he won't."

"Giving him that power though…"

"Trust me," she says, "I know better than anyone how scary that is. I mean, look at me, it's been nearly three years since The Dick Who Shall Not Be Named, and I still can't get over it."

If I thought what I went through with Thad was a roller coaster, it's almost nothing compared to what happened with Emilia and her ex. I don't blame her for not being ready, though I do think some of that has to do with a certain older hockey player…

"But I think of all people in the world, Lowell might just be worth putting your heart on the line for. You need to talk to him. Tell him how you're feeling. Be honest with him."

Truthfully, I think she's right. Hell, I *know* she's right. I can either put my heart out there and see what happens, or I can hurt and suffer alone.

I've never really been one to run from my problems, and I'm not about to start now.

"I will. I'll talk to him and I'll tell him how I feel. I—"

Another tidal wave of pressure hits me, and I press on my belly once again.

Emilia notices this time. "Are you okay?"

"Uh…yes." I wince.

"Are you sure?"

"Maybe? I'm cramping."

"How long have you been cramping?"

"Inconsistently? All day. Consistently? A few hours now, I think."

"A few hours…" she mutters. "Hollis, are you…"

"*Oh god.*" I lurch forward, my stomach *really* hurting now.

"Talk to me. Tell me what's happening. Is this like when you felt dehydrated?"

"No, no. This is…I…I don't know. Something else —*oh!*" Yet another wave of pain courses through me.

"Are you in labor?"

"No! Yes! I can't be! I don't even have my go bag packed!"

"Yes, I am certain that is *exactly* what your baby is waiting on—you to be prepared with your go bag."

"Not"—another wave, another sharp inhale—"helping, Emilia."

"Okay," she says, standing. "Up. We're going to the hospital."

"What?" I swat at her. "No. I'm telling you, it's nothing. I'd know if I were in labor. I'd—"

"Are you peeing on the couch?!"

I look down and—yep, there's a pool of fluid turning the light gray couch into a dark one.

Oh no…

"Uh, Emilia? I think I might be in labor."

"No shit! Come on, up. We're leaving."

She grabs me, helping me off the couch, tossing her purse over her shoulder as she rushes to get shoes on.

Another contraction hits me.

Oh my god.

Have I been in labor all day and not realized it? My stomach has been hurting worse through the day, but I shouldn't be in labor yet. I'm only 38 weeks. I still have time…

"Okay, let's go," she says, leading me to the door.

"My phone!"

"Your—where is it?"

I point to the couch, still trying to breathe through the pain since it's lasting for about a minute each time now. "I need to call…"

"Who? Who do you need me to call?"

"Lowell. I need Lowell."

CHAPTER 24

LOWELL

I'm about to be a dad.

Me.

I can't believe it.

"Can you not move this truck any faster? I know it's falling apart, but shit, you're driving like you're about to be a grandpa, not a dad."

We're fifteen minutes away from the hospital stuck in traffic. It's moving, but not fast enough.

Fucking game days.

I spare Harper a glare. "I can only go as fast as traffic."

"Bullshit you can. Get this baby up on the shoulder. Drive around."

"Do you have no sense of legalities when it comes to driving?"

"No."

"Remind me why I brought you again?"

"Uh, because you need me!"

I huff out a laugh. "More like because you *accosted*

me." I shake my head. "I don't know what it is with you Kelly women just butting into other people's business."

"Lowell, I swear, I *will* pinch your nipple if you do not just shut up and drive. I don't want to miss the birth of my niece or nephew!"

"And you think I want to miss the birth of my child?"

"Then drive!" she yells.

And I do.

I take Fiona right up on the shoulder of the road and I gas it.

We look crazy. Completely bonkers. What we're doing is illegal, and if the Comets aren't pissed that I ran out of the game without serving the second day of my healthy scratch, they'll really be pissed after they find out about this.

Harper's phone beeps with a notification.

"It's Emilia," she says. "She says they got her in a room and are waiting for the doctor."

"How dilated is she?"

"Ew, gross. I do not want to know how big my sister's cervix is."

"Harper…"

"Fine. It's a three."

"Okay, okay. So, we have time. That's good."

I slow the truck down as I inhale a sharp breath through my nose, then exhale through my mouth. I am out-of-this-fucking-world nervous. In fact, the last time I was this nervous was during the Cup Final. I would have never told the boys because they didn't need to see me sweat, but I was freaking.

That's nothing compared to this though.

"Are you doing Lamaze?"

"What? I've been watching some videos on YouTube. Sue me."

Hollis and I spent hours sitting in her bedroom learning breathing techniques. We'd practice until we'd start laughing.

Then we'd start kissing. And that always led to more.

"It's cute," she says. She reaches over, squeezing my arm. "You're going to be a good dad, Lowell."

I swear to fuck someone is cutting onions in this truck because tears spring to my eyes. I will them back, sniffling. If Harper notices, she doesn't say anything, and I like that she doesn't say anything.

"Are you excited to be an aunt?"

"Yeah. I'm going to be amazing at it. I already have a bunch of coffee and sugar at home."

"I'm pretty sure you're not supposed to *tell* the parents you're going to feed their child caffeine and sugar."

"Oh. Well, then, I definitely *do not* have any coffee or sugar at home. Absolutely zero."

I snort, then put my blinker on. I might be an asshole for driving on the side of the road, but at least I have *some* manners.

We pull into the parking lot and find a spot.

Then, I sit there. I sit there because I am having a

complete and total panic attack and oh my god I can't believe this is actually happening right now. I can't believe this is happening when Hollis and I haven't spoken in days.

I thought I'd have more time. I thought I might still have weeks to convince her I'm madly in love with her and want to spend the rest of my life showing her that.

"Lowell? You okay? You stopped Lamaze-ing."

I chuckle at that because it's not a real word and it breaks my tension.

"I'm okay. I'm just…"

"I know," she says. "I get it. But you need to pull your head out of your ass and get in there. It's a team effort and you need to support each other right now. Your girl—my sister—is waiting for you. Don't make her do this alone."

I grin at her. "You know, you wouldn't be too bad behind the bench. We could use a motivator like you."

"I know. Now, go tell my sister you love her."

"Yes, Coach."

"I'm looking for Kelly. Hollis Kelly."

"Who are you?" the nurse at the station asks.

"Her…*boyfriend*. And the father."

"Oh!" she says excitedly. "We were wondering when you'd get here. Follow me. I'll take you to her. I was just about to go do my check-in."

I follow the short nurse down the hall, Lamaze-ing the whole way down.

"Nice technique," she says over her shoulder, pushing the door open.

All my technique goes right out the window when I see Hollis lying in the bed. She looks…well, fucking gorgeous.

And in pain. Her eyes are squeezed tightly shut and she's holding her stomach, trying hard to breathe in and out of her nose. She does this for what seems like forever, and all I can do is watch.

"Oh, thank god! You're here!" Emilia says from behind me, walking into the room carrying two big cups full of ice, a soda tucked under one arm. "She's been dying for some water."

I don't think Hollis hears any of this because when the contraction finally subsides and she peels her eyes open, she looks completely shocked to see me.

"Cameron, you're—"

"I love you."

The words just fall from my lips. So quickly and so randomly even the nurse stops what she's doing and looks over her shoulder at me.

I ignore her, stepping farther into the room.

"I love you, Hollis. I'm *in love* with you. Like *really* in love with you. In fact, I think I might love you more than I love hockey." I take a few more steps, inching closer to the bed where she's staring up at me with wide, glassy eyes. "But I don't love you more than our baby, and I hope you can understand that."

She tucks her lips together, barely holding back a sob.

I can't take it. I have to touch her.

I rush across the rest of the distance in hurried steps and cradle her face in my hands. I look into those deep, dark blue eyes I can't get enough of, the ones I'll *never* get enough of.

"I just need you to know I love you, okay?"

She nods, and then, I kiss her.

I don't care if I'm not supposed to kiss her right now. I don't care if she's mad at me.

I have to kiss her. I can't stand here and *not* kiss her.

Luckily, she kisses me back with just as much fervor.

"You're here," she says when I pull away, a few tears slipping down her cheeks. I kiss those too.

"I'm here."

I kiss her again, and then once more for good measure.

"All right, Dad," the nurse says, laughing at us. "We need to check some stuff. Make yourself comfortable over there, all right?"

I move around to the other side of the bed, not letting Hollis' hand go as the nurse checks her over and makes sure everything is good.

"Well, we're moving along nicely. We're at a four now. We still have hours to go, so you just rest, all right, Momma?"

Hollis nods, already looking tired.

The nurse promises more people will be in and out, then leaves.

Emilia points to the door. "I'm going to give you two some privacy. Let me know when I can start playing some Bon Jovi."

"Bon Jovi?"

"You know, when we're halfway there and livin' on a prayer." She winks, then closes the door behind her, leaving Hollis and me alone for the first time in a week.

I blow out a breath and look over at her. Even a little sweaty and tired from the contractions, she's fucking stunning.

"Hi," she whispers quietly.

"Hi."

Then I just stare because she's here and I'm here and we're having a damn baby and I can't wrap my head around it.

I don't know how long we sit like that, but it's long enough that day turns to night and the moonlight shines in through the window directly onto her. She looks just like she did back in that garden, and I think I loved her even then.

"I'm sorry," I tell her, the words tumbling out of me. "I'm so fucking sorry. I'm an idiot for implying that you would do anything to harm our baby. I was just…"

"Scared," she supplies for me, nodding. "I know. I was too. I *am* too."

I blow out a breath because it makes me feel better to know she's afraid of this too. "I didn't plan on this, you know? I've been so against relationships and love and all the bullshit that goes with them for so long now. I've been putting hockey first and trying to forget that people have the ability to break you. But along the way, I forgot there's this whole other side to love. I forgot all the good parts, the ones that make you feel like you're on top of the world. I forgot all the parts that make it feel just as good as lifting a trophy over my head."

"Not just *any* trophy—the Super Bowl trophy."

I glower at her, and she giggles.

I fucking missed that giggle.

She sobers, squeezing my hand. "I know what you mean, Lowell. The thought of putting myself back out there after my divorce made me want to puke. Hell, it *still* makes me want to puke. I thought I'd have more time before I jumped into another life-altering thing. I thought I'd have time to figure out what went wrong before, to figure out what I want from life. But this"—she places her hand on her belly—"this *is* what I want. It's not what I planned by a long shot, but I've never been gladder for something to happen. And I'm glad it was you."

"I'm glad it's me too. Even if *we* don't work out together, I'm so glad my baby will always have you."

"It's a lucky baby, huh?"

"The luckiest." I kiss her hand, trying to ignore the way my hands are definitely shaking right now. "We are totally crazy for this, right?"

"Absolutely insane."

"That's okay. I've heard crazy is hot."

I wink, and she laughs.

"Miller?" I nod. "Figures. I can't believe we're here right now."

"I know."

"I can't believe you love me."

"I do."

"And I can't believe I love you too."

Her words shouldn't shock me. Not given the circumstances.

But they do.

They shock me because...this?

This is what Smith was talking about all along.

This is what was missing.

Them.

"Okay, wow. That is the *cutest* little bundle of squish ever."

Harper coos at the baby tucked safely in her arms. It's the same thing she's been doing for the last thirty minutes, not letting a single other person have a chance to hold her.

Hollis finally gave birth just after midnight.

Watching her deliver our child will forever be imprinted on my mind. Not just because it was completely disgusting—absolutely nobody can deny that —but because I swear it made me fall even more in love with her watching her power through that.

"Did you decide on a name yet?" Collin asks, looking over Harper's shoulder.

They've both been unable to stop staring.

"Miller!" the guy himself says. "It's totally unisex."

I roll my eyes. "It's not Miller, but we did settle on something. Do you want to tell them?"

"You can," Hollis says, looking exhausted but so incredibly beautiful all at once.

"Freddie Olivia Lowell."

Harper looks down at her brand-new baby niece. "Freddie. It's perfect."

They all clamor around her again, looking at the baby differently with her name.

"It *is* perfect, you know," Hollis says, grinning up at me.

"I know. And so are you." I wink.

"You know we can't have sex for like six weeks, right?"

"I'm aware…"

"So, then, why are you saying so many nice things?"

I lean down, pressing my forehead against hers. "Because I'm in love with you…*darlin'*."

She sighs. "I'll let you get away with it this time, but only because you gave me a beautiful little girl."

"Hell of a one-timer, right?"

"The best one-timer of my life."

"I love you, Hollis."

"And I love you…Cameron."

EPILOGUE

I was right.

About a month after Freddie was born, my mother packed up my childhood home, the one that held so many good and bad memories for her, and moved across the state to be closer to her new granddaughter. She is obsessed with Freddie.

Honestly, I can't blame her—I'm obsessed too.

If I thought I loved my little girl when she was just a little flutter inside of me, I was wrong. That love is nothing compared to watching my baby grow.

It's been nine months since my daughter was born, and I still can't believe I'm a mother. I can't believe I created and carried a little human and now I get to watch this baby flourish for the rest of her life.

Freddie laughs from across the room, the sound drawing my attention. Her tiny arms are outstretched toward her father, and I can't help but smile as he plucks her from her grandmother's grasp, blowing kisses into her chubby neck.

"You're so in love with him. It's gross."

I peek over at my sister, who is watching Lowell with her own grin.

"You're one to talk." I flick my eyes to her husband, who is standing next to Lowell, making faces at Freddie. "You're so in love with *him*."

"Yeah. I am." She sighs dreamily. "Can you believe this is where we are?"

"Not even a little bit."

"You're a mother."

"And you're a wife."

"And soon *you're* going to be a wife...right?" She lifts her brows in question like I'm harboring some sort of secret.

I laugh then flash her my hand. "Still ringless."

She sighs again, only this time it's less wistful and more out of irritation. "Fool."

These last two years have been the most tumultuous of my life between finding my ex-husband cheating on me, divorcing him, getting pregnant by my one-night stand, and then falling in love with said one-timer. Add in moving in with Lowell and adjusting to motherhood *plus* being a pro-hockey player's girlfriend on top of that, and —yeah, it's been a crazy ride.

But if Lowell were to ask...I'd say yes in a heartbeat.

Much like how I thought I loved Freddie before she was born, if I thought the love I had for Lowell was strong before our baby came into this world, I was dead wrong. Watching him become a father has taken my feelings for him to a whole different level.

I don't think I'll ever forget the first time he had to leave for a road game after Freddie was born. During the birth? Not a single tear, but leaving Freddie's side for the first time? He lost it. He cried for ten minutes before he finally got out the door to catch the flight. His coach reamed him a new one, but Lowell swears spending those extra minutes with his child was worth it.

That was the first moment I fell even more in love with him. There have been about a hundred other moments since then that have made me fall even harder.

Like the time he got home at two AM after an away game then insisted on being on nighttime duty with Freddie, who was struggling to sleep through the night.

When we went for a date night and my boobs started leaking through my dress, even though he wasn't wearing an undershirt, he took his dress shirt off so I could cover up. He didn't even care that he had to go shirtless under his suit jacket throughout the rest of our dinner.

And even now, today, he's been walking around wearing that silly shirt I bought for him the first Christmas we spent together, not the least bit embarrassed by the bold *WORLD'S HOTTEST HOCKEY DAD* letters across it.

As if he knows we're talking about him, Lowell's eyes find mine, and a huge grin lights up his face. He stalks toward us, Freddie in his arms. She reaches out for me, but Harper steps in, stealing her away.

"What? You don't want Mama. You want Auntie Harper! Aunts are way cooler than moms," she says, brushing her nose against Freddie's as her niece laughs and burbles out some nonsense.

"Moms and aunts are cool and all, but uncles are where it's at!" Collin declares, stealing Freddie from his wife's arms. He plops her down onto her playmat, dropping to the floor and stacking up blocks as Freddie watches with giddiness. She knows exactly what's coming.

Harper and Collin are still firmly against having their own children, but that doesn't mean they aren't complete constants in Freddie's life. The number of times I've had to beg my sister to spend time with my own child is a little ridiculous if you ask me. They are both over here at our home nonstop, stealing away all of Freddie's attention.

"Honorary uncles too," Rhodes adds, sitting on his knees next to them and picking Freddie up to recreate a scene from *Godzilla* as he crashes her through the blocks.

Harper, Ryan, and my mother all sit back on the couch, laughing as they take turns playing blocks and monsters with her. It's her favorite game.

There is not a single soul in this room who would ever dare to say Freddie isn't loved. It's so obvious by the way she's garnered the attention of each person, including the always grumpy Smith, who is admittedly a little less grumpy these days.

Lowell slides his arms around my waist, dropping his chin to rest on my head.

"They're so in love with her," he says, pressing a kiss to my temple. "Just like I'm so in love with you."

"That was incredibly cheesy. Say it again."

He laughs. "I'm so in love with you." He drops his lips to my ear and splays his hand across my still flat stomach. "All three of you."

I might not be harboring secrets about an engagement, but I am harboring another one.

I'm pregnant.

We didn't plan it, but we were significantly less shocked this time around.

"Do you think they'll love the second one as much as the first?" I whisper to him.

"I don't know how they couldn't. We make cute babies."

I grin at Freddie, her dark curls bouncing as she giggles with her whole body. "That we do."

"Do you think *we'll* love the baby just as much?"

"Yes. But I have to admit, I'll love you a little less."

My brows pinch together, and I look up at him. "You will?"

"Yes, but only because I'm going to have to make room in my heart for another girl. It's nothing personal."

My heart skips a beat. "I think that's fair, even though there is no way it's a girl."

He lifts his brows. "You really want to bet against me on that given my track record?"

"You had a 50/50 chance of being right. It's not that impressive."

"No? Well, if you're not impressed with that, let me show you something that *will* impress you." He pushes his hips into me, and there's no mistaking the feel of his cock against my ass.

"Lowell!" I hiss out. "We have company!"

"Uh, yeah, you do, and I'm going to pretend I didn't just witness all that." Emilia waves her hand in our direction as she passes us, plopping down on the couch between Miller and Smith.

Miller slips his arm across the back of the cushion behind her but removes it just as fast when he catches sight of the glare Smith is directing his way.

I tuck my lips together, trying not to laugh.

"Can we send them all home yet?" Lowell asks.

This time I do laugh. Lowell's always been a notoriously private person, to the point that only like five people on the team even knew where he lived, but now we have almost a constant rotation of people in and out, especially on Sundays when we host brunch whenever the Comets are on a home game stretch.

"They just got here."

"So? I'm ready to have you alone again."

"You just had me alone."

He runs his nose along my neck. "It wasn't enough. But to be fair, it'll never be enough."

"I'm sure you'll get tired of me eventually."

"Not a chance." He presses a kiss to my neck. "Forever, remember?"

"I remember."

"Do you? Because if you need a reminder, I will gladly sign a legally binding agreement to make sure you don't forget. You know, one with like rings and shit."

I tip my head up, meeting his green eyes, which are usually so certain and so confident.

"Did you just propose to me?"

"No. Yes. Kind of?"

"Kind of?"

"I mean…" He runs his tongue along his lips. "Is that… Is that what you want?"

It doesn't happen often—in fact, I've only seen him like this twice—but Lowell's nervous.

"Is that what *you* want?" I echo.

"I asked you first."

He grins, and I roll my eyes.

He chuckles at that. "Yes. It's what I want."

"Because I'm pregnant?"

His brows pull together. "No. I… No. Actually, I think I've wanted it since the moment we met."

"You wanted to marry me when I punched you?"

"What can I say?" He shrugs. "I like 'em crazy." He winks. "What do you say, darlin'? Want to get married?"

"Are you serious?"

"Completely."

I blink up at him, stunned.

"Don't mess with me…" I warn, narrowing my eyes.

"I would never. I already know you got a mean right hook."

"Cameron…I'm serious."

"So am I."

He steps away from me…and drops right down on one knee. He shoves his hand into his pocket, producing a gorgeous teardrop ring.

My hand flies to my mouth because I was so *not* expecting this today.

"I love you, Hollis, more than I've ever loved anyone —aside from Freddie—in my entire life. Marry me."

"I…" I glance over at the others, who are all now watching us intently, monsters and blocks completely forgotten. I look back down at Lowell, who is grinning up at me with a smirk that is just entirely too confident.

He knows—because *of course* he does—that I'm going to say…

"Yes!"

Everyone in the room explodes into a chorus of joy.

Lowell presses a quick kiss to my belly before pushing up to his feet, swooping me into his arms, and peppering me with kisses.

"Have you been planning this?" I ask him.

"This exact moment? No, but I've had the ring for a while now."

"How long is a while?"

"Nine months."

"But that's…"

He's had it since Freddie was born.

"Someone wants to say congrats to Mama and Dada."

I grab Freddie from Harper, snuggling my baby close. Lowell wraps his arms around both of us, and I think this may be my favorite moment of ours yet.

"Ma…ma."

I gasp, tears welling in my eyes. "Oh my gosh! She said *Mama!*"

"Now say *dada*." Lowell tries to coax it out of her.

"Ma…ma," Freddie says again, smiling.

"Say *dada*."

She just grins up at him.

"Ha! Mama wins. Mama's the favorite," I taunt.

"That's okay, little darlin'," Lowell says, kissing her head but keeping his eyes on mine so I can see the pure love swimming in his eyes. "Mama's my favorite too."

I lied.

This is my favorite moment of ours.

Thank you for reading **ONE-TIMER**!
I hope you enjoyed Lowell & Hollis.

Want more Carolina Comets?
SIN BIN (Smith & Emilia) is up next!
One-Click SIN BIN Now >

Want more Lowell & Hollis?
Sign up for my newsletter for a bonus scene!

Looking for more Collin & Harper?
PUCK SHY is available now!

OTHER TITLES BY TEAGAN HUNTER

TEXTING SERIES

Let's Get Textual

I Wanna Text You Up

Can't Text This

Text Me Baby One More Time

INTERCONNECTED STANDALONES

We Are the Stars

If You Say So

HERE'S TO SERIES

Here's to Tomorrow

Here's to Yesterday

Here's to Forever: A Novella

Here's to Now

Want to be part of a fun reader group, gain access to exclusive content and giveaways, and get to know me more?

Join Teagan's Tidbits on Facebook

Stay on top of my new releases!

Sign up for my newsletter

ACKNOWLEDGMENTS

My husband, the Marine. By the time this book hits one month old, we'll have been together for 15 years. Some days, I can't believe we made it. But others? Others I knew we would all along. I love you.

Laurie. Thank you for always being there when I need you and for keeping me on track.

My mom and sisters. Thanks for always being there when I need to vent. I love you all.

My editing team. Literally couldn't have done it without you.

#soulmate. I couldn't do this without you and your constant support. I love you and thanks for always flashing me your titties. *wink*

The Bloggers and Bookstagrammers and BookTok. Your support is unmatched. Your hard work doesn't go unnoticed by me. Thank you for everything.

My Tidbits. You're my favorite people to hang out with on the internet.

Reader. Thank you for trusting me with this new-to-me trope. I hope you loved Lowell and Hollis as much as I did when writing them. I can't wait to tackle my next new-to-me trope in SIN BIN.

With love and unwavering gratitude,
   Teagan

TEAGAN HUNTER is a Missouri-raised gal, but currently lives in South Carolina with her Marine veteran husband, where she spends her days begging him for a cat. She survives off of coffee, pizza, and sarcasm. When not writing, you can find her binge-watching *Supernatural* or *One Tree Hill*. She enjoys cold weather, buys more paperbacks than she'll ever read, and never says no to brownies.

www.teaganhunterwrites.com

Ingram Content Group UK Ltd.
Milton Keynes UK
UKHW011305120323
418437UK00004B/255